Gray Back Broken Bear

Gray Back Broken Bear
ISBN-13: 978-1517421014
ISBN-10: 1517421012
Copyright © 2015, T. S. Joyce
First electronic publication: September 2015

T. S. Joyce
www.tsjoycewrites.wordpress.com

All Rights Are Reserved. No part of this book may be used or reproduced in any manner whatsoever without written permission, except in the case of brief quotations embodied in critical articles and reviews. The unauthorized reproduction or distribution of this copyrighted work is illegal. No part of this book may be scanned, uploaded or distributed via the Internet or any other means, electronic or print, without the author's permission.

NOTE FROM THE AUTHOR:
This book is a work of fiction. The names, characters, places, and incidents are products of the writer's imagination or have been used fictitiously and are not to be construed as real. Any resemblance to persons, living or dead, actual events, locale or organizations is entirely coincidental. The author does not have any control over and does not assume any responsibility for third-party websites or their content.

Published in the United States of America

First digital publication: September 2015
First print publication: September 2015

Gray Back Broken Bear

(Gray Back Bears, Book 4)

T. S. Joyce

ONE

The *thwack, thwack* of Easton Novak's ax driving into birch logs echoed through the quiet clearing.

In a smooth motion, he pushed the split wood off into the growing pile beside him and stacked another wide log onto the old chopping block. After swinging the ax handle behind him, he lifted it in the air and blasted the blade through the wood. Again and again, he swung his ax until he had enough for a cord of firewood. That wasn't the point of this, though. The purpose wasn't to prepare for winter. The cold months were behind him, after all. It was early spring and he already had enough wood to last him a month of deep snow, plus a couple of cords to sell.

The point was to settle the animal that snarled constantly deep inside of him. He had work to do. Oh, he saw how the other Gray Backs looked at him. The girls, Willa, Gia, and Georgia were more tolerant, but he still scared his crew on some level.

As he should.

If they knew what was really going on inside of him, Creed would've put him down years ago.

This wasn't working. All of the physical exertion wasn't settling him enough. It never did. He'd have to Change. Maybe fight and bleed, too. The restlessness that washed over him lately was suffocating. His bear was struggling for breath inside of him, clawing and tearing. He didn't know what the damned thing was fighting against. And he sure as shit couldn't tell anyone else what was wrong. He couldn't even figure out his own animal.

The other Gray Backs called themselves misfits, but none of them could even touch the baggage he carried.

The flutter of wings sounded behind him, and Easton threw a narrow-eyed glare over his shoulder, but the branches of the old pine that shaded his trailer were empty, save needles and pine cones.

Gritting his teeth, Easton peeled his shirt off and wiped the sweat from his face. With an irritated sigh, he tossed his shirt onto the railing of the stairs that led to his front door, then pulled another log onto the chopping block.

Another flutter of wings, and he was going to kill the fucking bird who was scratching at the memories he wanted to keep buried. No, the memories that he *needed* to keep buried, or his bruin silver bear was going to rip him to shreds on his way out.

Flap, flap, scritch, scratch.

She wasn't real. Not real, not real. The raven was a ghost, just like Tessa had been Jason's ghost. The bird had left him alone all these years, but now that he'd admitted to seeing Tessa, the ghost raven was back to torture him.

He cracked the blade down the center of a log.

Flap, flap.

"Stop it," he murmured.

He laughed as the knee high grass tickled his frail shoulders.

Easton blinked hard and slammed the ax down. He couldn't do this again. Not today.

Flap, flap.

"Leave me alone," he growled out.

Dad picked him up and swung him around

and around. Easton laughed louder as Dad tickled him and rasped his beard across his face. Silly Dad, always ready to play.

"Dinner," Mom yelled from the front porch of their cabin. Mom. Home. Safety. Everything was cherry. Mom made a pie for desert. The sweet sugar granules smelled so good on the wind. Sugar and wheat, and his stomach growled, ready to eat.

"My hungry little bear," Dad said, tucking him under his arm and tromping through the tall grass.

Easton smiled up at the tree branch where his raven sat, watching him. Her head was cocked, and she blinked slow as Dad carried him up the stairs. Easton waved just before the door closed behind them.

Hungry little bear.

"I said stop it!" Easton's legs buckled under him as he dropped the ax.

Flap, flap.

With a snarl, he pulled his knife from the sheath on his belt and turned. In one swift motion, he flipped the blade and threw it at the branch where the ghost raven sat. The knife sunk into the bark, and the flapping of wings filled his head. She was gone, but a single, shiny, black feather floated this way and that in front of the trunk of the pine. Easton drew back in horror. "You're not real."

She wasn't. Couldn't be.

He lurched forward and picked up the feather. It felt real enough, soft and light. Smooth as he ran his finger down the length of it. The feather even smelled like her—his raven. Chills blasted up his arms as he searched the branches above.

He would have to burn her things.

He would have to set fire to the trinkets he cherished the most.

Chest heaving, Easton climbed the stairs to his trailer and threw open the door. He kept the gifts she'd brought him under his bed in an old, plastic tackle box. Each section was labeled with a year, and filled with the tiny treasures she'd dropped in places for him to find.

He sank to his knees and yanked the lid open. Hair berets, rubber bands, paperclips, and anything small that glinted in the sun. The last compartment was empty.

Easton swallowed down the loss that filled him and pressed the feather into it.

She was a ghost, and he couldn't keep her. Not anymore. He owed it to his crew to move on.

Every trinket held a memory, and he would have to watch them burn, one by one.

Not today, though.

Today he wasn't strong enough, but maybe tomorrow he would banish the ghost raven.

TWO

It was him.

Aviana King clutched her arm to her middle, wishing for the pain to stop.

A sob clawed its way up her throat.

It was him. Her bear. Easton.

Easton, the one she'd grown up with.

Easton, the one her heart had latched onto.

Easton, the boy who broke.

It had to be him. His eyes were that same bright green color she'd never seen on another person. He looked different now. Harder. Feral. He felt different, too. Scarier. The power that rolled from his shoulders had washed over her raven form and terrified her. Her feathers had lifted uncomfortably from her skin just being that close to him.

Now, he was one of the wild bears her people spoke of. One of the dangerous ones.

Tears blurring her vision, she studied the long slice under her arm. Blood streamed from it like a crimson river. He'd become better with blades. Much better than when he was a boy.

She hated the bears, but she envied their healing abilities. Raven shifters didn't repair themselves so easily.

Easton had hurt her.

Clutching her arm, she curled in on herself, naked in the woods and miserable at the memory of his wild face.

The sweet boy she'd known was gone.

The flutter of bird wings drew a gasp from her lips. When she looked up into the evergreen canopy, it was only a woodpecker, not a raven. Still, it was a stark reminder that she shouldn't be here. This was against all the rules, and if her people found out she was so close to the bears, she'd be shunned.

Aviana stood, ignoring the jolting pain in her arm. Her pile of clothes was neatly folded over a young tree's low-hanging branch to keep the forest floor bugs from them.

She dressed quickly and jogged down to her car that was at the end of a deer trail she'd followed in. She drove a trusty white sedan whose easily muddied color and shoddy suspension were not made for the rocky terrain and pothole-riddled roads in these mountains. More proof she didn't belong in the woods. Not anymore. She'd been ripped from them long ago and had fought tooth and nail to move on.

And dammit, she'd led a good life. A safe one with friends and family and adventures. She'd never wanted for food or clothing, and she'd been able to follow her dreams of becoming a school teacher. So why hadn't she been able to stop thinking about Easton after all these years?

With a long, steadying exhalation, she slid behind the wheel. She turned the car around and headed for the main road that would lead to her childhood home.

He'd been here all along. She'd gone back to his territory once a couple of years ago, but it had been apparent Easton had left it long ago. She'd been riddled with such guilt when she'd left, she had forced herself to stop searching. It was the promise she'd made to her father. The first promise she'd ever broken.

Even now, another overwhelming wave of remorse washed over her. Aviana gripped the steering wheel and willed herself to stop feeling bad. If anything, seeing him like that was for the best. Now she could stop thinking and obsessing about him. She could stop imagining him in his adult form, fantasizing that he was as happy and fetching as she'd thought he was when they were younger.

Now, equipped with his angry snarl and the vitriol with which he flung that knife to kill, she could get over him. She could move on and accept Caden's proposal. She'd already quit her job at his request. All that was left to do was say yes to the small ceremony he'd proposed. She was of breeding age, and Caden had been kind to offer her a place at his side.

She was lucky. He was handsome and cunning, and his proposal had been highly sought after. He was perfectly nice. *Perfectly nice.* She could bear him children and raise them, create the perfect nest for the family she would build with Caden.

Her life would be easy.

Her life would be planned.

Another tear rolled down her cheek.

Her life would be perfect.

A flawless, emotionless existence because she'd given her heart away years ago to a broken boy with a silver grizzly inside of him.

And now that boy was dead.

After driving miles of winding backroads, Aviana pulled her car to a stop in front of the cabin she'd grown up in. It was abandoned now, but the house from her memories was beautiful. Mom had set up summer rose gardens all around the porch and hung potted plants from the rafters over the porch swing. Inside had been small, but tidy and comfortable. It had been a home, and one she'd connected with more than any other that followed.

Now, the logs that made the walls had faded to gray and splintered. The thick grout between the lumber had cracked and chipped. The roof sagged, and on the north side, moss had grown over the wooden shingles, giving it the look of a fairy cottage. Some of the wooden floor boards were missing and split on the front porch, and the railing was broken and sagging off the side, but that didn't bother her as much as what had happened to the inside.

Leaks and rot had ruined all of the furniture her family had left behind. The plumbing didn't work anymore, and her parents' bed was nothing but soft wooden shards in a pile on their bedroom floor. The place smelled musty and dank, and the lack of electricity made staying in this place rough.

The windows had been broken, and seeing it like this now, the cozy home from her childhood memories wavered.

As a child, she'd felt safe here.

As an adult, she felt vulnerable and exposed.

She wouldn't be here long, though. Just another night, and she'd go back to Rapid City and give Caden her answer. She'd kept her suitor waiting for a year. Longer than she had any right to make any man wait. She wasn't plain, but she was no beauty. Her jokes made her people uncomfortable. Her human friends at the school she'd worked at had laughed, but she was inept at deciphering between pity laughs and genuine amusement. Caden was a good man, and she was lucky he'd offered to give her a home.

Maybe if she just kept telling herself that, it would feel true.

Aviana took a drag of the musty air inside the door and shook her head. This place had gone to ruin without someone here to keep it alive.

It reminded her of Easton.

Another wave of disappointment clogged her throat as she opened her laptop. Thirty percent battery left, but it was enough to say goodbye to Easton in her own silly way.

She made her cell phone into a hot spot and pulled up Cora Wright's pro-shifter Web site. This was where this whole adventure had started. There was a link to a list of registered bear shifters in the country.

This was where she'd found Easton. How could it not be him? She'd never met anyone else with the unique name, and he was a bear shifter to boot, registered with a crew of notoriously violent, aggressive, unsavory bears called the Gray Backs.

She skimmed through his registration information again. Six-two, lean build, green eyes, dark hair. Silver bear. Surname: Novak. She hadn't known that from before.

Aviana Novak.

Stop it.

She was destined to be paired with Caden. She would be his perfect match. Everyone said so.

From there, she clicked over to Jason Trager's social media page. None of the other Gray Backs had one she could find.

A jolt of shock zinged through her as a picture of Easton showed up at the top of his feed. In it, Easton stood in between Jason and a woman with medium-length red hair, obviously dyed and straightened so thoroughly, it spiked out of a high ponytail. They were all smiling, even Easton. His was smaller than the other two, and a little bewildered, but it was there.

Aviana frowned and tried to connect this face with the ferocious one he'd worn when she'd seen him.

Underneath the picture, Jason had typed hashtag sammysbar, hashtag cteamcocaptains, hashtag willawonka, hashtag releasethebeast, hashtag beastonbromance.

Beaston?

The nickname certainly fit the monster who'd cut her with a knife today.

He seemed to have friends if this picture was anything to go by. Aviana leaned back in her chair and crossed her arms. She squinted at his smile. He was very handsome with his face relaxed like this—more like the boy she'd known. So why did he live in a trailer separate from his crew? She'd done her spying on them, and the Gray Backs lived a good three hundred yards away. And it was plain as day the man was fighting some mighty big demons the way he was chopping that wood so relentlessly. A terrifying growl had been constant in his throat.

But then again, she'd seen what happened to him. She'd come here hoping he turned out okay after everything, but he hadn't. The circumstances of his life had turned him into a monster.

She was disappointed.

There it was. Okay, she was disappointed that he hadn't been strong enough to find happiness. The Easton she'd known was invincible.

She'd come here in hopes she could convince herself he had turned out all right despite all that shit that had happened to him, but he hadn't. And now she would have to go back and live this empty life with Caden, and all the while she'd wonder *what if?*

What if she'd been able to stick around for him when they were kids?

What if she'd come back to find him earlier before he'd turned dark?

What if she'd ever revealed herself as a person—a real flesh and bone friend—instead of just an attentive raven?

What if she was the reason he was so lost now?

Her low battery signal flashed and the screen went dark.

"No," she whispered as Easton's slightly

baffled smile faded to black.

She couldn't go now. Aviana shook her head and closed her eyes at the thought of leaving. Easton, or Beaston, was terrifying. Hell, his entire crew brought shivers up her spine. Bloodthirsty, violent apex predators who obliterated everything in their path. They would eat a peacekeeping raven like her for breakfast and pick their razor teeth with her bones.

But Easton's life was now more mysterious than it had ever been, and she had to heed whatever was drawing her to him.

She would see this thing through.

She had to.

Because a life of what ifs was no life at all.

THREE

Easton pulled his knife from the sheath at his hip and cut in one swift motion the zip tie that bound a trio of thick cable loops.

Matt watched him thoughtfully. He did that a lot—tried to figure Easton out. It was annoying, but then again, everything was annoying.

Matt shifted his weight and leaned back on the giant stack of processed logs behind him. "I bet the real reason Clinton left is because you never made a knife for him."

Easton huffed a laugh and shook his head. "Clinton left because he's a D-team dick. His bad decisions had nothin' to do with me."

"Think about it," Matt said. "He begged you for one from the first time he figured out you made them. Maybe if you gave him a knife, he'd come back to the Gray Backs."

Easton looked down at the long, sharp blade of the knife he always carried. He hadn't made Clinton a knife because he hadn't deserved the effort. Willa, Gia, and Georgia had.

Easton ran from the house to the shed where Dad was working. In the branches of an old alder tree, the raven cawed. He grinned and waved to her as he blasted his little legs faster toward Dad's workshop.

Shaking his head to ward off the memory, Easton said, "Clinton won't ever come back. He don't belong with us."

"Where did you learn to make your knives anyway?"

In a flutter of wings, the raven swooped down from the towering alder and landed on the splintered windowsill of the shed. Easton gasped as he got to see her up close for the first time. Slowly and carefully, he padded toward the window. She was carrying something shiny in her beak, and when he approached, she set a small bent paperclip down on the ledge. He thought she would fly away, but she didn't. She only watched him while he picked up the small gift and turned it in his hands.

"Thank you," he whispered.

"That raven sure likes you," Dad said. He

was leaned against his work bench watching the big, black bird with his arms crossed over his chest and his head cocked.

Easton looked at her proudly, so close he could almost touch her. Pocketing the paperclip, he said, "She's my best friend."

A soft sob whipped around on the breeze, easy for his sensitive hearing to pick up.

"Mom's crying."

Dad narrowed his eyes and turned his back to continue sharpening a thin knife blade. "Well, let her have some time alone. She'll get over it."

Easton sidled up to the table and fingered a set of clamps. "What's wrong with her?"

With a sigh, Dad turned and squatted down to eye-level with Easton. "Son, your momma's going to have another baby."

A smile spread across Easton's face as he thought of a brother or sister to play with. Another sob carried on the wind from the house. He frowned.

Dad ruffled his hair. "Your momma's scared. She fancies she has the sight and can see her future. She thinks the baby will be hard to have, but she's just being emotional. Human women are like that. Soft and full of tears."

"She doesn't want the baby?"

"She will." Dad stood and blew on the newly

sharpened blade of the knife he was making.

But Easton knew all about babies. They had raised pigs all his life, and he'd seen how the boar got the sows with piglets. "If Mom didn't want a baby, why did you put one in her?"

Dad tossed him a hard look and went back to examining the sharpened silver. "Someday you'll understand. Your momma is flighty, and I don't want her leaving us. Now she won't. Not with two cubs to raise. Sometimes you have to make the hard decisions for the people you want to keep around."

Easton winced as he put his weight on his bad leg, the one Willa had ruined when he'd Turned her without her consent. All because he wanted to keep her around. Dad had been wrong. Making decisions for women got his bones snapped, and then Creed had ordered the Gray Backs not to set his broken leg. He'd done a shitty job of trying to fix it himself, and now every step he took, man or bear, hurt. His limp would always hurt.

"Hellooo," Matt drawled, waving his hand in front of Easton's face.

Red, boiling rage took his middle, and he snapped his teeth hard at Matt's hand. Matt flinched back and cursed. "I'm not challenging," he said, hands raised in surrender as he stepped away, never giving him his back.

"Beaston!" Power cracked in Creed's voice as he yelled from under the skyline where he was securing new cables. "Don't you fucking do it today. Damon finally lifted our numbers. He's trusting us more. Don't ruin this shift for us."

Easton's bear squirmed inside of him, burning him from the middle out in desperation to escape. He wasn't even mad at Matt. The memories made it so he couldn't help himself. Fighting made them go away.

With a snarl, he turned and skidded over the ledge of the landing. Below, there was a steep mountainside cluttered with felled lumber the Boarlanders had cut down for the Gray Back Crew to strip and load for shipment to Saratoga. The terrain was steep and uneven, and one wrong misstep meant a lumber avalanche that would go careening down the hillside, picking up steam and demolishing anything in its path. He loved this job. There was always an edge of danger in everything he did. Here, he could focus better than anyplace else on earth. Which was pathetic since he still fought the other Gray Backs all the fucking time. Irritation bubbled inside of him as he headed to where Jason was standing on a stack of logs and writing numbers on his clipboard. Clad in a yellow hardhat like his own, Jason was easy to spot.

"Hey, you okay?" Jason asked.

"I'm fine."

His dark eyebrows shot up as he shook his head and went back to scribbling on the clipboard. "Lay off my hide today, will you? I'm still sore from our row yesterday."

"Sorry," Easton muttered as he climbed onto the pile next to his friend. And he really was. He liked the Gray Backs more than any other people in the world, but that hadn't stopped his need to fight with them.

"Creed will kill me soon," Easton said, dragging his gaze to where his alpha was climbing into the machinery under the skyline.

"He won't."

"He will."

"Easton," Jason said, slapping the clipboard against his thigh. "Anyone messes with you, they'll have to claw their way over my cold and lifeless body to do it." Jason inhaled slowly and leveled him a look. "Breathe."

Easton drew a slow, deep breath and felt the fire inside of him cool by a fraction.

"There you go. Now think about it. Creed has put a lot of time into rehabbing you. He didn't kill you when you Turned Willa, did he?"

Easton shook his head, still uncertain about his future.

"And now Creed would have to answer to the girls if he put you down. Willa would filet him and suck on his marrow, Gia would boot him out of their trailer, and Georgia would shoot his ass. Nobody's giving up on you, so you don't give up on you either. Okay?"

The flutter of wings in the tree line distracted him.

"Easton," Jason murmured, gripping his shoulder. "Okay?"

"Yeah," Easton said with a jerky nod.

"Good. Now make it today without bleeding us, and me and you will go into town later and grab a beer."

"Creed won't agree to that."

"He will if it keeps us on track with our numbers today." Jason jumped over a pile of beetle-infested, dead lodgepole pines and made his way up toward the processor. "Chest up, eyes ahead, and focus, Beaston. No bleeding today, and I'll buy."

Beaston. He couldn't decide if he liked that

nickname or not. It certainly fit his inner monster, but it was also a stark reminder that he was different. More abrasive, more combative, less in control.

With a sigh, he reached in his pocket and pulled out the bent paperclip his raven had gifted him all those years ago. It hadn't been Matt's fault for dredging up memories. It was his own for tucking this trinket in his pocket this morning.

His dad had scoffed at Mom for thinking she had the sight, but he'd been a fool to shrug off things he didn't understand. Mom was special and could see things no one else could. Easton hadn't understood until he got older, but she'd gifted him with the ability to see things in the beyond, too. He'd seen the ghost of Jason's first mate when the others hadn't been able to.

Easton lifted his gaze from the paperclip in his hands to the raven in the tree across the clearing.

And now he could see his ghost raven.

Dad had been wrong about a lot of things.

FOUR

Aviana sat stunned on the branch, trapped in Easton's gaze.

He'd kept the paperclip.

She remembered every trinket she'd ever found. It was a blessing and a curse to a raven. So many baubles bounced around in her head, but her memory was impeccable, and she wasn't able to let go of even one.

That had been the first gift she'd ever given to him. She'd done it to get his mind off his Mom crying inside the small cabin he shared with his parents. She'd given it to Easton to show that she cared, and then he'd gone and rewarded her by telling his dad she was his best friend.

That day, she'd given him the folded paperclip and her heart.

From the branch she'd dug her claws into,

she could hear his low, rumbling growl before he ripped those eerie green eyes away from her and looked back at a man climbing down the mountainside toward him.

Tiny heartbeat pounding, she bounced sideways down the limb and hid behind the body of the tree. The tree was hurting, and its spirit almost faded to nothing. Pine beetles had suffocated and starved it. She could feel its pain, but that was nothing compared to the ache of watching what had transpired with Easton and the rest of his crew.

He was struggling. An outcast in a crew of outcasts. It seemed he was in trouble with his alpha, but she couldn't figure out why. It was apparent he was on the verge of a Change, too. His eyes had always blazed like a demon's when he was close to a Change, but in the last two days, the glow had been constant.

She liked that man, the one with the clipboard who'd dared to grip Easton's shoulder despite the terrifying rumble in his throat. He'd tried to make Easton feel better about things she was helpless to understand.

It was suddenly overwhelming, the years that stood between them.

She'd missed most of his life.

There was tragedy in that.

A trio of heavy steel cables, hanging from a line high above, blasted down the mountain side. There was staggering power in the machine that pushed the cables toward Easton and the other Gray Back. Matt? It was hard to put their faces to the pictures on Jason's social media when they were wearing yellow hard hats.

Easton and Matt worked to tie the long cables in loops around logs, three at a time. Then they gestured with a thumbs up to the alpha above them on a ledge, and the logs were dragged up the slope at a frightening speed. Tirelessly they worked, hooking logs, always running around, jumping, sure-footed as mountain goats. Easton sported a limp now, but it didn't seem to hinder his work. Pain slashed through her chest when she saw him wince, though.

Perhaps his limp was from the bear trap.

It was March and still cool up in the mountains, but Easton only wore a white T-shirt and threadbare jeans with holes in the knees over heavy work boots. His pants clung to his tapered waist and powerful legs. When she was younger, she thought Easton the most dashing boy she'd ever laid eyes on, but Easton the man was a work of art. His cut arms pressed against the thin fabric of his shirt, and as the day wore on and he worked up a sweat, his shirt clung to the defined muscles in his back. And when he linked his hands behind his head while waiting for the cables to come flying back down the hillside at him, she could make out ripped abs as the damp material clung to his torso. His skin was tanned from the outdoor manual labor, and at one point, he smiled at Jason who was working a big machine that stripped the limbs off logs and leveled the ends. Easton's teeth were white and straight. If he would only smile deep enough, she'd be able to make out the shallow dimples he'd had when he was a boy. The ones he used to flash her before everything got so messed up. Before he was broken.

Easton was stunning. Masculine, lithe, powerful. Full of barely checked aggression as he worked alongside Matt, who seemed to dig at Easton's nerves when he spoke. Easton was terrifying and beautiful, like a tornado she'd witnessed from a distance when she was ten. She couldn't take her eyes off him.

Her heart rate wouldn't settle down, and it left her feeling dizzy. She gripped her tiny talons into the bark more securely as Easton rolled his neck and wiped his cheek on the shoulder of his shirt.

This feeling right here—the breathless, stomach-dipping, bewildered one—this was what falling for a man should feel like. Perhaps the elders could've convinced her this feeling didn't exist if she hadn't already felt it. Caden had formally asked to court her, and for twelve long months, she'd been trying to force herself to feel something—anything—for him.

But after seeing that bent paperclip on Easton's palm today, any hope of settling for Caden was lost.

Easton as a boy had tempted her heart.

Easton as a man was ruining her for anyone else.

****

As the sun sank down, half-hidden behind the mountains, the alpha waved his crew up to the ledge he stood on. They chuckled at something Jason said, all but Easton, who stared at the ground as if it held the answers to all the secrets in the world.

The rest of the crew loaded into a fat-tired charcoal gray truck, but Easton got behind the wheel of an old, beat-up white Ford truck and took off behind the other pickup alone.

Aviana followed, desperate to watch him as long as she could manage without him noticing. Getting close to him near his trailer wasn't an option anymore. Not with his impeccable aim with knives. But out here, where there was more room and more trees to hide her, she felt safe to observe him, as she'd done for so many hours in her youth.

She flitted from tree to tree as the Gray Backs bounced and bumped down switchbacks and old dirt roads that led them toward the Grayland Mobile Park. Finding her courage, she circled high above as Easton parked his truck beside the one his crew rode in, then he strode through the woods to his mobile home. In the trailer park, the other Gray Backs reunited with their mates. Some were playful, like Matt and Willa, and others sweet, like Jason and Creed with their women. Those made her look away and swoop back toward Easton's territory.

He had no one to come home to.

Sorrow and hope churned in her middle. Even among the Gray Backs, he lived a solitary existence. Perhaps he didn't want a mate. Or perhaps he couldn't handle one after everything that had happened. Or maybe, just maybe, he hadn't found the right woman.

That last part lit her up with longing.

She was too chicken to show herself. She

hadn't been able to do it in her youth, and the rules hadn't changed. No one could know raven shifters existed. Especially terrifying, murderous bear shifters.

But Easton was different.

From high above, she watched him stride deliberately into his trailer. The door banged closed behind him.

Was he different?

Her arm was still cut from where he'd hurt her, and he'd seemed barely in control of himself at his jobsite.

Maybe she was just fooling herself into thinking he was the boy she'd grown up with. His wild eyes said that part of him was long gone.

But...the paperclip.

Baffled, she flapped her wings and caught an air current that pushed her toward the cabin she'd grown up in. She needed time to think about all of this. And something else was weighing heavy on her mind now—something that made her cringe to consider.

She needed to call Caden.

Being the careful raven she was, Aviana searched a perimeter around her house before she Changed back into her human skin. It wasn't painful or slow like it was for some shifters. Ravens were lucky in that respect. She just tucked her animal away in the span of a moment, and her feathers disappeared like magic. The stairs sagged dangerously under her feet as she padded up to the house, careful to avoid the nails that stuck out of the floor boards. Her phone had enough charge, so she scrolled through her contacts and hit the call button when she found Caden's number.

She let off a long, steadying breath as it rang.

"Hello?" Caden asked.

"Hi. It's me."

"Aviana? Where are you? I've been calling for two days, looking for you everywhere. You can't do this shit. I need to know where you are at all times, or this doesn't work."

She'd only been gone two days so his reaction was overblown.

"I think that's a problem for me. I mean, one of the problems. I don't like that you need to keep tabs on me. And I don't like that you made me quit a job I love." Oh, she was in it now. "And I don't particularly like…you." Her voice faded off on the last word. She wasn't trained in being so direct with a man. "This isn't what I want. A pairing between us isn't going to work."

Caden was quiet for so long she checked her phone to assure herself he hadn't hung up.

"And you've thought this through?" he asked in a low, steely voice that brought a shiver up her spine. "You've thought about your place with our people, and you are fine with your rank staying at the bottom where you've always been? You've thought about the fact your refusal of my courtship will keep your family at the bottom?"

Aviana swallowed the lump in her throat as tears stung her eyes. She loved her parents and didn't want them to be beneath anyone, but she couldn't live a lie to elevate their status. She would only grow to resent them. "Y-yes."

"Yes, what?"

Aviana gritted her teeth and hated herself as she whispered, "Yes, sir."

"Who is he?" Caden asked. The emptiness of his voice echoed on and on in her mind.

"He's not you." She hung up the phone as a sob crept up her throat.

She'd done it, and part of her was proud she hadn't just given into what was expected of her. She was proud she'd stood up for a life she wanted. But the rest of her was scared shitless. Caden was important, and taking his last name would've given her family a much easier life. More respect.

But she wasn't giving up the comfortable life Caden could provide for another male raven, or God forbid, a human mate. She was giving it up for Easton, a monster grizzly with little apparent control who had tossed a knife at her as though she was less than nothing.

She was betraying her people by choosing a bear, but she couldn't help herself now. Easton was hers—had always been hers—and coming back here to find him even more broken than when she'd left him had sealed her fate to his.

Aviana didn't know how, but she was going to find the courage to talk to him.

FIVE

She couldn't do this.

Aviana took a long pull of the fruity cocktail she'd implored the bartender to make "extra potent." She'd overheard Jason telling Easton he would take him out for a drink, and after seeing the picture of him and Easton and whoever Willa Wonka was, Aviana was pretty sure they would grab that drink at hashtag sammysbar. The Sammy's Bar in question was a hole in the wall establishment on the main strip in Saratoga, complete with dim lighting, sticky floors, and mismatched chairs around scuffed wooden tables. A pool table sat in the corner, and a stage sat empty up front. The coaster for her drink advertised the Beck Brothers played live music every weekend.

Jason and Easton probably wouldn't show.

Good, because again, she really couldn't do

this. Her heart was pounding double-time, and her hands were clammy. Twice already, she'd almost dropped her drink on the table because she was shaking so badly. If she did this, talked to Easton, it would change everything. It would put her at risk of being shunned, and would put her, a lone, frail raven, in the path of the most volatile group of badass grizzly shifters in the country.

"'Scuse me, miss," a man with thinning hair and whisky breath said from the barstool beside her. "Can't help but notice you're here alone and dressed like you're ready to party."

She swung her disgusted gaze to him. "Piss off." She cringed and slapped her hand over her mouth. That was really rude and not her at all. The alcohol was definitely talking now. "I mean, piss off…please?"

The man snorted and turned to his friend on his other side.

That was a sign it was time to go. Aviana sucked down the rest of her drink and stood, only to gasp and fall back onto the barstool the second she saw the door open.

They were here. And not just Jason and Easton either, but the entire Gray Back Crew filtered in through the door.

Oh, great hairy balls, what was she going

to do now? Panicking, she slunk with her back to the bar to the very end where she eyed a rear hallway and exit sign.

"Gotta release the kraken," Willa Wonka announced.

"Geez, Nerd," Matt said, shaking his head with a smirk on his face. "Just say you have to take a piss."

"Don't tell me what to do," the spunky redhead said through a flirty grin, pointing at her blue-eyed mate.

Oh God, oh God, oh God, the three Gray Back women are walking this way. Act natural.

Aviana slurped extra hard on the last watered down drops of her drink and wheezed when a lemon seed shot through the straw and pelted her deep in the esophagus. She couldn't breathe! Gasping, she clutched her throat and tried to drag in oxygen.

"I got this, sugar tits," Willa said. She grabbed Aviana around the stomach and nearly cracked her rips in a quick, one-shot Heimlich. The lemon seed shot out of her throat and onto the bar top. Aviana turned around, mortified.

Willa reached forward and grabbed her boob. "Honk, honk, you're welcome."

"Are you okay?" a very pregnant brunette

asked, gripping Aviana by the elbow as Willa sauntered off, clutching her tie-dyed purse and humming to herself.

"Uh." Besides the fact that she'd just been felt up by a werebear? "Yes. Thank you."

"Good," the woman said kindly. As she walked off behind the other two, Aviana tried to place her face from pictures on Jason's social media. Gia, human mate of Creed, she remembered.

She swung her gaze to the bar on her other side where the rest of the crew were sidling up and ordering drinks. From here, she could see Easton lean forward, a slight frown marring his striking features. When he turned his head, his gaze grazed over her.

Gasping, she froze. She couldn't do this— nope, no way.

Melting to the floor, she crawled around the corner of the bar so her movement wouldn't catch Easton's attention as she made her escape.

"Lose a contact?" Willa asked from the bathroom door she was holding open for the others.

"Oh!" Aviana stood and pressed her back against the wall, hopeful that Easton wouldn't hear Willa talking to her and come to see what was going on. Spread out like a starfish, she closed her eyes and sidled down the hallway wall.

When she opened her eyes to see how close she was to the exit, Willa was standing in front of the bathroom door, arms crossed as she stared at her. "Yep, I can still see you." She narrowed her eyes and canted her head. "You a shifter groupie or something?"

"No. Yes! I like bears. They seem very…nice."

"Liar. You sound and smell terrified."

"Right. I'm just going to find the bathroom."

Willa pointed to the door directly behind her. "There she be."

"Okay." Aviana's words were coming out all breathy as her throat closed around them. "Thank you."

Willa followed her inside, and now she was trapped between her and the other two who were washing their hands. A werebear sandwich, and how fitting that she was the meat. A whimper clawed its way up her throat.

"Dudette, are you going to pass out?" Willa asked, a sliver of worry infiltrating her tone.

"Maybe?" Aviana said as she pressed her shoulder blades against the tile wall. So unsanitary, but right now, the grimy wall was the only thing propping her upright. "I should go."

"I think you should put your head between your knees," Gia said, casting her a worried look.

"Yes," Aviana whispered, sinking to a squatting position on the tile. She put her hands behind her head and waited for the lightheadedness to fade. Only now, she was completely vulnerable to the bears. Georgia, though she was even prettier in person than in the pictures on Jason's posts with her wild hair and freckles, felt dominant. Willa, too, and now they were probably going to eat her.

A gentle hand rubbed her back, and when she looked up, the curvy park ranger smiled kindly down at her. "I used to be afraid of bears, too. We're not that bad, though."

Willa snorted, but Gia elbowed her sharply.

If Aviana didn't ask now, she would never build up the courage again. Not after this disastrous night. "Can I ask you a personal question?" she asked Willa.

"Oooh," Willa drawled out, tossing her head back. "Sorry about the boob grab, but I'm totally into dudes."

"What?" Aviana asked, utterly confused.

"I like the pene." Willa waited, eyebrows raised high. "The bratwurst? The talley whacker, the trouser snake, the one-eyed serpent, the dong, the long schlong, the tadpole shooter—"

"Willa," Gia said, fighting a smile. "I think she gets it. And I also don't think she was hitting on you."

"You're very pretty," Aviana whispered in a fraidy-cat voice, "but I was going to ask you about Easton Novak."

"Beaston?" Willa looked utterly shocked.

In fact, they all looked shocked.

"What do you want to know about him?" Georgia asked carefully.

"Is he...is he seeing anyone?"

"Honey, you'd be better off hitting on me. You aren't exactly Easton's type," Willa said, leaning on the counter.

"W-what is his type?" she stumbled out.

"Serial killer." Willa got elbowed by Gia again.

"I can see the appeal because he's very handsome," Gia said low, "but you are barking up the wrong tree with that one."

"More like barking up the wrong forest," Georgia said, rubbing her back. "That man isn't meant for a mate, and especially not a woman as…soft…as you. You seem very nice, but a shy girl like you would sure have her work cut out for her with a man like Easton. Best you get him out of your head."

Georgia flashed her a sympathetic smile and stood.

And as Aviana watched them file out of the bathroom, her heart sank to the dingy tile beneath her heels.

Get him out of her head?

If she could've, she would've forgotten about her affection for Easton a long time ago.

Deflated, Aviana washed her hands, then made her way back into the bar. It wasn't so intimidating to stay now that she'd made an ass of herself in front of half of the Gray Back Crew. The night couldn't get much worse, as highlighted by Easton's indifferent glance over at her as she left the hallway. He didn't recognize her at all. Which, yeah, she got it. She hadn't ever shown him her human side, and raven shifters didn't have a smell unless they were in their animal forms. Not like furry mammal shifters did. To him, she was just another plain human hanging out in the bar he frequented.

She wanted to buy another drink to soften

her sorrows, but the Gray Backs were talking and laughing it up at the bar, and she couldn't force herself to get that close to them again. Peeing her pantaloons in fright after that utterly embarrassing scene in the bathroom would just be the cherry on top of the night.

The table in the darkest corner near the stage looked like the perfect place to watch Easton for the last time. What a failure. She'd come in here thinking she could actually talk to him, and the closest she'd gotten was talking to some of his crew, who probably thought she was a complete ninny.

Easton sat stoic in the middle of the laughter at the bar. He was picking apart a napkin with a slight frown drawing down his dark eyebrows. Every once in a while, he sipped a drink, but it was apparent this wasn't his scene or he had some serious thoughts on his mind.

She was going to leave without seeing his dimples.

Her eyes blurred with pathetic tears, and she clutched her purse closer to her lap.

A massive man blocked her entire view of the bar. She arched her neck back to take in his full height. Dark hair, soft, sympathetic dark eyes, and two drinks in his hands. "Before you ask me to sit down, know that I won't hit on you. I'm here on a reconnaissance mission only."

Aviana sniffled and wiped her damp lashes. "Aw, what the hell. Will you sit?"

The man took the seat beside her, freeing up her view of Easton again. He set a red, sweet-smelling drink in front of her and took a long pull of his own. With a sigh, he said, "Woman, you've set your sights on one tough target."

"I don't know what you mean."

"Yeah, you do. Why Easton?"

She shrugged miserably and took a pull from the cranberry vodka he'd brought her. "He reminds me of someone I used to know."

"So, why don't you go talk to him?"

"Because I'm a chicken." She smiled sadly and swung her gaze to the behemoth. "It's in my inherent nature."

"Your inherent nature," he repeated in a thoughtful voice. "So, if you never talk to him, what will happen?"

"I'll never know him."

"And if you talk to him?"

"Worst case scenario, he rejects me in front of all of his terrifying friends, scars me emotionally, I give up on ever talking to another man again, draw into myself with fear of being humiliated, push away everyone in my life, move out to some reclusive cave, and live on beaver meat and wild berries until I become an unrecognizable hermit with questionable hygiene and an imaginary pet fox."

"Well, that was graphic and not at all what will actually happen when you go over there and say hi to Easton."

"Oh, I'm not doing that. Chicken, remember?"

"So chug that drink and dig down deep. Find that badass I know is hiding in there somewhere. Hike up your big girl panties and march your sexy ass over there and make him notice you."

"Sexy, hmm." She clinked her drink against his. "Flattery gets you everywhere with me, mister giant."

The man chuckled and jerked his chin at her drink. "Bottoms up, chicken. The Beaston awaits."

He was right. If she left without talking to him, she'd always be disappointed in herself for giving up before she even tried. Feeling reckless, she slurped the drink down and stood. "I'm going to do it."

"That's the spirit."

"I'm going to go talk to him."

"You can do it."

She straightened her tank top over her jeans and pulled her purse over her shoulder. She turned to leave, but hesitated. "I'm Aviana."

"Nice to meet you, Aviana," the man said with an easy smile. "I'm Kong."

Kong. What a strange name. "Thanks for the pep talk."

He nodded once, his dark eyes dancing. "Anytime."

Aviana squared her shoulders and set her eyes on the crew at the bar top.

She was definitely going to do this.

SIX

A woman cleared her throat delicately behind Easton. He turned on the barstool to tell her "Gray Backs only," but the words got stuck in his throat the moment he saw her.

She was a wisp of a woman. Taller than tiny Willa only by a couple of inches, and with a fine bone look that said he could snap her arm without any effort. Her skin was tan, a smooth olive tone that made her clear-water blue eyes even more striking. Long, dark lashes matched straight black hair.

When he'd seen her come out of the bathroom, he'd taken notice. For an instant, she'd looked familiar. Or not looked, exactly. She *felt* familiar. Stupid fucking thoughts.

The woman lifted her overly big eyes to him, then dropped them to his work boots as if his shit kickers were the most interesting thing she'd ever seen.

His crew grew eerily quiet. All except Willa, who muttered, "Oh, shit," and grabbed the woman's trembling hand to steady it.

Too late to hide her fear from him, though. If he couldn't tell she was shaking in those sexy little pokey-heeled shoes she was wearing under those tight jeans, he sure as shit could smell how terrified she was. Acrid. Bitter. He swallowed hard and waited for his bear to slash its way out of his skin.

But his inner monster stayed put.

In fact, the longer he sat staring at the strange girl in front of him, the more his bear shrank back inside of him, as if he was stunned. Or scared. Huh. Scared of this wood sprite?

Easton angled his face away from her suspiciously but never took his eyes off her downturned face.

"I'm Aviana Marie King." She ghosted a glance to him, then back to his boots. "I saw you from over there, and I think you're very handsome." She gasped a tiny sound, too low for human ears, but it perked his senses right up. "You're cheekbones are sharp, and your nose straight...regal...big muscles...and your eyes...I like those." A tiny whimper escaped her as she clamped her mouth closed.

Easton looked to the faces of his crew, one by one. When he got to Jason, he growled out, "Is this a joke?" It had to be. No one had ever penned him as handsome. They avoided his gaze and shielded their children, but never once had someone called him what this strange woman had. Jason must've dared her to come over and talk to him. Now it made sense why she was this nervous.

"Definitely not a joke," Jason muttered. "I've never seen her before."

The woman was clutching her fist at her side, and her other hand was grasping Willa's like a lifeline. She seemed to be waiting for something.

Oh. The manners the girls had been teaching him. "I'm Easton." His voice came out a gravelly snarl, and the woman's scent went from scared to petrified. Shit. "Sorry."

She looked up through those long, dark lashes. "Sorry for what?"

He shook his head, baffled. "I don't know."

The tiny human straightened her spine and lifted her chin. "I want to buy you a drink."

"But I already have—"

Jason shook his head, eyes wide.

"Okay," Easton said, rubbing the two-day

scruff on his face self-consciously. Manners. "Thank you."

Aviana huffed a relieved, shaky sigh and released her death grip on Willa's hand. Then she sat on the barstool Jason offered her right next to Easton. *Right* next to him. She smelled like vanilla. Not the artificial kind in a bottle, but the real kind to cook with. He liked vanilla. Her hair was clean and shiny and looked soft as silk, and she had a face he wanted to stare at. Cute nose, high cheekbones, and round, innocent eyes. She didn't look like she had anything wrong with her, but she was talking to him. Maybe she was soul-sick. "How old are you?" he asked.

"Ooooh," Willa said from behind him as if he'd said something wrong.

"It's okay," Aviana said with a brief smile to Willa. "I'm twenty-eight."

"Me, too. Do people call you Ana?"

Her soft lips turned up in a smile as she shook her head. "No. But you can if you want to."

"I want to." It was shorter. Easier than Aviana. Gray Backs gave nicknames. Nerd. Griz. Ranger. Beaston. He would give this one to her for tonight. She seemed nice. Frail and breakable, but nice.

Ana ordered him another beer and one for herself. She grimaced when she took the first taste, though. She didn't like it, but she forced it down her throat, sip by uncomfortable sip. She tipped the bartender a five dollar bill. Maybe she came from money, or maybe she was just that nice.

"Where are you from?" Easton asked. It wasn't small talk. He was shit at small talk. He just wanted to know more about a woman who would brave the Gray Backs and call him handsome.

"Rapid City. I was a teacher there. Kindergartners."

Easton took a long draw of his beer. She was smart then. So why was she talking to him? "Why aren't you a teacher anymore?"

Her cheeks turned the most appealing shade of pink. "I quit for a man."

His bear snarled inside and scratched tauntingly beneath his skin. "Why would you do that?"

"Because he asked me to, and I didn't understand that I could say no at the time. I thought he was it for me."

"Your mate?"

She couldn't meet his eyes anymore. She nodded her chin once. "I guess you could call him that."

Easton wanted to kill everything. "Why aren't you with him now?"

"Because I didn't want to be with a man who asked me to quit something I loved."

Pride blasted through his chest, and he smiled as he took another drink of his beer. "Good." Not so frail. Not so fragile.

The soft sound of giggling brushed his sensitive ears, and he turned to where his rowdy crew had moved off down the bar. Willa and Georgia both gave him thumbs up and big, confusing smiles, and when he looked for Gia—because she was pregnant and he liked her close so he could help Creed protect her—she was waddling double-time, round belly leading the way, toward the jukebox in the corner. He narrowed his eyes suspiciously.

"I met Willa and the others in the bathroom," Ana said softly, following his gaze. "They seem nice."

"Then why are you so afraid of us?"

That part he couldn't figure out. If she was a shifter groupie, she'd be more brazen. Instead, she was clutching her drink and sitting at the opposite edge of her barstool.

"Because you're a bear shifter."

"And you're scared of shifters?"

She nodded.

He stared at her for a long time. She was beautiful, smart, and shy, and obviously terrified to be this close to him, so why was she talking to him in the first place?

"Is this some sort of dare or bet?" he asked, scanning the room. Kong lifted his beer in the corner from a table he sat at with his Lowlander Crew, but other than that, no one was watching them that he could tell. "Are your friends taking pictures or something? I don't do social media, and I'm rarely on the Internet, so that shit won't hurt me."

"I'd never hurt you," she said on a rushed breath.

He jerked his gaze back to her. Truth. Every word she'd just uttered had been laced with honesty. Who the fuck was this girl? And why wasn't his bear a snarling mess inside of him like he was every other minute of his life? He set the beer bottle down and backed off the stool. "Why would you want to talk to me? And don't give me the handsome line. I know what I am, and I know what I ain't. Mixed up, bloodletting berserker at the mercy of my alpha's patience. But you're too good to be sitting next to some crazy lumberjack grizzly shifter."

Ana was clutching her purse now, and as she slid off her chair, she looked like she was going to cry. *Human women are like that. Soft and full of tears.* She was little and helpless, like he used to be, and now his protective instincts were kicking in for a woman he couldn't afford to get attached to.

She wasn't a Gray Back. Would never be a Gray Back because all the boys were mated. *Except you.*

Easton took a step back. His bear had the right of it—afraid and quiet around this dangerous little creature.

Easton spun to escape Sammy's Bar—to escape Ana—but Willa stood in his way, a pissed off little hellion. She blasted her fists on her hips. "Ask her to dance."

"What? No."

Willa's usually happy brown eyes narrowed to dangerous little slits. "Yes, she's soft, Easton, yet somehow, she found the courage to come over here and talk to your scary ass. I like her. If you hurt her feelings, I'll break your fucking leg."

He made an angry clicking sound behind his teeth. "You already broke my leg." And he had the permanent limp to prove it.

Willa's eyebrows wrenched upward. "You

have two legs. I can play that game twice."

He growled at her and turned around. "Do you want to dance?" he muttered to Ana, his words gravelly.

Ana's pretty blue eyes had somehow gotten even bigger. They took stock of half her fucking adorable face now. "I think so?"

"Great." Easton grabbed her hand and tried not to crush her fingers and break all her bones as he led her to the empty dancefloor.

This was the part where Creed, Matt, and Jason usually fought their mates. Empty dancefloors with one couple drew too much attention, but Easton gave exactly zero fucks who watched him. Beaston was his name and town crazy was his game, and he'd accepted the stares a long time ago.

Gia had picked a slow song, and with a frustrated snarl in his throat, he turned around and pulled Ana's hand to his shoulder, then held her other one out to his side and swayed back and forth.

Ana was holding her breath and had gone pale as a sheet. And now he wanted to kill whatever was upsetting her, but unfortunately, the only danger to her was him. His head was so mixed up. He shook it hard and tried to focus on not touching her too hard. She would turn to ashes and blow away in a stiff wind if he did.

"Breathe," he demanded.

She inhaled deeply as a tremble shook her shoulders.

"I'm not going to hurt you. I won't, so you don't have to be scared."

Her hands were miniature against his, and for the first time when he straightened to his full height, he got the chance to see how tiny she was next to him. It was almost laughable. He had a foot on her and a hundred pounds of muscle, at least. She squeezed his hand, and he drew up short. Wait, he was touching her.

"What's wrong?" she asked low, her eyes so big and vulnerable. She gave away every emotion with them.

He'd stopped dancing, so he picked it up again. Side to side as he held Ana as gently as a dried sand dollar.

She cleared her throat and looked around. Everyone was staring, but he didn't care. Ana, however, seemed to wither under the attention. "You dance very well," she whispered.

"Does that surprise you?"

"Yes. I thought a man like you would step on my toes and lose his rhythm, but you're quite good."

His face stretched into a quick smile, there and gone at her compliment. Handsome and a good dancer, and Ana the Mystery was giving him all the compliments a man like him never thought he'd hear. He would reward her kindness with an explanation.

"My mom taught me to dance."

Surprise flitted across her face, and her full lips molded into a smile that stole his breath from his chest. "I didn't know that."

What a strange thing to say. Of course she didn't know that. She didn't know him.

"I was seven. She taught me in our living room and told me, "To make a fine man someday, you need to learn to dance with a woman." *To hold her proper and gentle, as a real man ought.* That part had been meant for Dad, who sat at the table and glared at their lesson. Mom loved to dance to an old record player in the living room. Dad never had danced with Mom that Easton had seen.

"She was lovely. I mean...she sounds lovely." Ana's breath shook harder as she stepped closer to him and rested her cheek as light as a paintbrush stroke against his chest.

She would hear it now. Ana would hear how hard his heart was beating just being this close to her. He should pull away. Hide. But when he looked at the exit, Willa was standing in front of it with her finger jammed at him, shaking her head. Fuck.

At least Ana hadn't asked what happened to Mom. He liked the tiny human more for it. She wasn't digging too deep as he'd seen the other shifter groupies try to do when the Boarlanders were at Sammy's trying to get their dicks stroked. So many questions. Ana didn't do that, though. Ana was nice and gentle.

Why was his bear still so quiet?

"Where did you learn to dance?" he asked, just to distract her from his heartbeat battering her face right now.

"Not from my parents. When we moved to Rapid City, I went to public school for the first time. There was this school dance, and I was so nervous. I'd been homeschooled all my life, and there were so many kids it was intimidating." Her voice shook on every word, but it was getting stronger. "A boy in my class asked me to dance. It was very stiff and scary, but he showed me what to do. And afterward I felt accomplished and brave."

He didn't like thinking about her dancing with anyone else. Which was stupid and territorial, and he had no right to get possessive over her. Ana wasn't his. Still, he rested his chin on her head so she wouldn't see him curl up his lip in a snarl for the boy who had asked her to dance.

Something strange was happening. Ana stopped shaking, and she went all warm and soft in his arms. She stepped even closer, pressing her body flush against his. Vanilla. Her hair was silk against the rasp of his beard. Such a contrast to him. Good Ana. Bad Beaston. Another song came on. Another slow one. Gia was controlling the jukebox now and threw a middle finger at one of Kong's lowlanders for complaining. Was Willa crying? No, couldn't be. Just a trick of the lights playing with his eyes. Ana felt so good against him, but now that she was so close, she'd feel how excited he was. How could she not? His dick was hard as a rock between them.

"I have a boner." Perfect. That would set the mood. Idiot.

"For me?" Ana asked. Was that hope in her voice? She looked up with those ensnaring eyes.

God damn, she felt good pressed up against his dick like this. "That was supposed to scare you away."

"It doesn't. I like that you say what you mean."

He liked that about her, too. Honest notes in all her words and shit, she felt good. Good, good, good. Ana, his Ana. He wanted her under him, on top of him. Fuck.

"I have to go," he murmured. A deep frown hurt his face. He didn't want to leave her, but she was as fragile as a dry leaf, and he wasn't the beast for her. *Quiet bear, where are you?* The lights were too bright in here.

"Okay," she said, disappointment pooling in her big, blue eyes.

His guts hurt. He'd done that, disappointed her, but it was best this way, leaving now. He would only disappoint her more if she knew how fucked up he really was.

Bowing, he kissed her hand like mom had taught him, then he strode for the door and past Willa whose sad eyes matched Ana's.

Don't look back.

He blasted through the door and out into the dusty, gravel parking lot.

He turned and glared at the door as it swung closed behind him. A long growl rattled his chest, and there he was—the beast in his middle.

Every step Easton took away from the bar

hurt, but he forced himself to walk to Jason's truck and dropped the tailgate. He sat on it and looked at the stars. If he was lucky, the others would be headed out here now to go back to the Grayland Mobile Park with him.

"Did I make you angry?" Ana asked from behind him.

Easton jumped. Shit, how had she snuck up on him?

She was shaking again, badly. This made no damned sense. Ana was obviously terrified around him, yet she kept approaching him.

"You make me feel like a monster." It had been meant to hurt her, and his words did. That much was obvious by her face falling. More gutting him, more ache. She shouldn't have this kind of power over him. No one should. She was going to draw out his bear.

But...his inner grizzly had stopped snarling again.

"You're not a monster," Ana said low as she stepped carefully over a pothole in the gravel. "And if you ever say that around me again, I won't talk to you anymore." As the brave little human dragged her gaze back to his, she looked angry. Smelled angry. Vanilla and fury. "You're good."

"I'm not."

She eased closer and rested her hands light as feathers on his knees. "You *are*." Her tone had turned to grit and steel.

Easton froze under her touch. Ana was fragile, and he would hurt her if he moved. Settling in between his legs, she cupped his face gently with her palms. She searched his eyes and smiled. "I liked dancing with you. And when we talk, I get butterflies in my stomach."

"I make you sick?"

"No," she said through a laugh. He liked the sound. Soft and feminine, her giggle tinkled like a bell. "I mean, you make me have flutters in my stomach because I like the way you make me feel."

"You're pretty." He cleared his throat and swallowed hard. He could do that part better. "I think you're the prettiest girl I've ever seen." There. Better. That felt right.

She smiled again and stroked her thumbs across his cheeks. "I always wondered what it would be like to have you say that to me."

Easton gripped her wrists and shook his head, confused. "I don't understand you."

Ana stood on her tiptoes and rubbed her cheek softly against his. Silk against the rasp of his scruff. More proof of how different they were. He was a jagged river rock, and she was the gentle water.

Now it was Ana who was steady as Easton's heart raced and his breath shook. She was so close, so warm, touching him. *Him*. He wasn't a stupid man, and he knew he would never see Ana again, but for tonight, for right now, he was going to enjoy a woman pretending he was something more than a monster.

His breath came in shallow pants now as the corner of her lips brushed his. Closing his eyes, he threaded his fingers through her soft hair and gripped gently. *Don't go.* The next time she eased back to brush her cheek against his, he pressed his lips to hers as gently as a delicate woman like Ana deserved. His bear pushed for more—harder, faster. *Taste her!* But Easton forced his hands and lips to be easy. Easton had told her he wouldn't hurt her, and he wouldn't. Not now, not ever.

He stifled the urgent growl in his throat so he wouldn't scare her. Ana angled her face and sucked gently on his lips. Fuck, he wanted more. Needed it. He nipped softly at her mouth, grazing her with his teeth, and she let off a quiet moan that did disastrous things to his middle. Burning, fire, dick so hard.

He just wanted a taste. A small one. Just one.

As her lips moved against his, he touched the closed seam of her mouth with his tongue. A request, not a demand, because Ana was good, and she should make the decision whether to let a beast like him in.

Her lips parted, and he brushed his tongue against hers. Fuck, he was being too rough with her hair. He dropped his hands down to her waist and dragged her closer, pressed her against his erection because she felt right and warm between his legs.

He kissed her harder. Not his fault—his bear's fault. The animal was in his head, pushing to be closer to Ana now. She slid her arms over his shoulders and tightened around his neck, pulling him nearer. *Don't hurt her, Bear. Be gentle.* Fragile, delicate Ana. He was an avalanche, and she was a hummingbird. Courageous little creature. Sexy.

She rolled her hips against his, and he gritted his teeth, pulling away from their kiss as he rested his forehead against hers. "Ana," he warned her shakily. She was undoing him.

"I like when you call me that." She hesitated, then kissed him once more, a soft peck that plucked at his lips. With a smile, she backed away. "Your crew is waiting to leave."

Easton dragged his gaze away from her and over his shoulder. The Gray Backs were coming out of the bar.

Ana headed toward a white car. *Don't go.* She unlocked it, then slid in behind the wheel. When the engine roared to life, she rolled down the window. *Goodbye, Easton.* He knew it was coming. The words that would rip his insides out.

"I'll see you tomorrow, Easton," she said with a shy smile and pink cheeks.

Stunned, he stood from the tailgate and watched her drive away.

Ana had made him feel almost normal tonight, but that wasn't the only gift she'd given him.

She'd given him his first kiss.

SEVEN

Easton sat on the back porch of his trailer and watched the progress of the sun as it sank down behind the mountains. He fingered the strand of frayed, black silk ribbon he'd taken from the raven's treasure box this morning before work on the landing. The day had been hard as his focus had drifted this way and that between thoughts of Ana and the meaning of the black ribbon that he'd tucked deep inside his pocket.

It served as a reminder. Ana was frail like Mom had been. She wouldn't survive a man like him, so it was best that her words, "I'll see you tomorrow, Easton," had been nothing more than a pretty lie. She didn't even know where he lived.

He pulled the length of ribbon through his fingers. A raven's sympathy.

"Where has he gone off to?" Mom asked, hands on her hips as she squinted against the setting sun that threw the front yard into the golds and oranges of autumn.

Easton had just hit his first grizzly growth spurt and was almost as tall as his human mother now. He shrugged and pressed his hand against her belly where the undulating was the strongest. It was a boy, a little brother. He just knew it. "Maybe he fell asleep somewhere."

Mom inhaled deeply. She was tired lately and had trouble moving around. Her feet swelled at night, and she was short of breath, but Dad didn't let her ease up on the chores. Not this close to winter.

"Next year, can I go to school with other kids?" he asked. He wouldn't dare mention it to Dad. He already knew that answer.

Dad would say, "Boy, you know what you are? You gotta bear inside of you, and humans can't be trusted with that kind of information. We stay out here in the woods for survival. Get that cockamamied idea out of your head. School." And then he'd spit in the grass because he always did that when Easton asked a dumb question. He spat on the ground the same as he used a period at the end of a sentence. Discussion closed.

Mom was softer, though. She understood how lonely it was out here.

She smiled sadly down at him and squeezed his shoulder. "Things were going to be different, Easton. I had plans for you and me, but the baby derailed them. Maybe someday, but not now."

Plans? Troubled, Easton looked out over the yard again as his senses picked up something that lifted the fine hairs on the back of his neck. Something was wrong in their woods.

"Dad?" he called, stepping off the porch.

Movement stirred the dry grass in the brush just behind the tree line.

Easton trotted forward at the sound of a pained groan, and Mom followed as she was able.

Dad appeared from behind the trees, stumbling and slow. Easton couldn't understand what he was seeing, though. Dad's head was crooked on his shoulders.

"Oh, my God," Mom whispered in horror. "Easton, don't look." She covered Easton's face with her hands and yanked him to a stop. "I said don't look!" Mom was sobbing now. "Go back into the house!" she screamed as she ran for Dad.

Dad fell to his knees, body convulsing as he toppled over sideways.

Easton approached slowly, horrified as Mom cried over him. His neck had been snapped. No.

"Russ," Mom cried. "What do I do? Can I reset it?"

"No," Dad wheezed.

"I don't understand. I don't understand! How did this happen? No. It'll be okay. I'll fix it. Easton get back in the house! Don't look!"

Maybe Dad had fallen out of a tree or over a ravine. His shifter healing had worked, but froze his broken neck at the wrong angle. Some injuries were too bad for even shifters to survive. All his life, Dad had taught him not to get careless with his healing. Easton heaved breath as Mom wept and positioned herself above his body. She was going to re-break his neck.

"Mom," Easton said, voice thick. He shook his head. "It won't work."

"Mae," Dad choked out.

"What is it Russ. What is it?"

"Mae...I'm sorry." A long last breath escaped his lips, and his eyes rolled closed.

"No!" Mom screamed. She pulled hard on Dad's head, but breaking a neck wasn't so easy. Not for weak humans. "Don't leave me here! Don't leave me!"

Mom's agony tore at his own burning heart. Dad. Easton dropped to his knees in shock at how broken he looked. How grotesque he looked in death with his bulging neck. He'd come back to say goodbye. Tears streamed down his face as he buried his head against Dad's stomach. He was still warm and smelled of life. "Dad," he murmured, gripping his clothes and dampening his shirt with tears.

The raven fluttered and flapped in the branches above, but he couldn't pull himself away from Dad's body. He and mom sat like that for a long time, crying against him until he grew cold and stiff.

Easton had never heard someone break before, but he knew whatever was happening to Mom was awful.

Mom shook his body. "I was going to take him and leave, and you wouldn't let me! He can control his bear now. We could've made it! And you ripped that away from me. And now you've left me? You've left us here in this hell you created? You can't." She clenched his shirt in her fists. "You can't, Russel. Do you hear me? Easton will be all alone!"

All alone?

So many tears. Mom's face leaked on and on, long after Easton had run dry. He eased away, lay against a felled tree and watched Mom cry. The evening shadows had turned to darkness as the sun sank behind the mountains. The light from the cabin was the only thing that lit the clearing. Not even the moon was full enough to lend them adequate light. Mom stood up, muttering strings of words that didn't make any sense at all. They meant nothing. Maybe they weren't even words at all.

Mom didn't see him anymore as she stood and began gathering wood. Her eyes had gone empty, and her tears had dried on her cheeks. She couldn't see as well in the dark as him, yet she found wood as though she had the forest memorized.

Silently, he helped her. He was small yet, only eight, but Mom was pregnant and heartbroken, and whatever she was doing right now, he could lighten her load. Alongside her, he dragged wood into the clearing in front of their cabin until the early hours of the morning. She didn't answer him when he asked questions, so he gave up trying.

And when the first streaks of pink brushed the horizon, Mom asked him to help her drag Dad's body to the pile of wood. And then she lit a match and watched him burn.

Easton buried his face against Mom's side

and clutched her dirty dress, unable to watch the fire consume his dad. "Why?" *he asked.*

Mom inhaled deeply and asked, "Easton?" *as if she'd only just noticed him clutching onto her.*

"Why are we burning him?"

"Because, my boy. Your daddy would haunt these woods for always. You and I see the ghosts, Easton. We'll burn his belongings and put salt around the house next. That's what you do, Easton. Can you remember that?"

"Yes, ma'am," *he said on a choked breath. He could smell Dad burning.*

"Repeat it for me."

"Burn the bones, burn the belongings, salt."

"That's a good boy." *Her voice sounded strange—dreamy—as she watched the flames.* "You'll need to do the same thing for my body."

"Don't say that."

"Promise me, Easton. Don't let me haunt you."

And that's when he felt it.

Mom's belly was pulled up tight like a drum.

Easton gritted his teeth against the pain in his middle. He could still smell the smoke from the funeral pyre. The ribbon had done that. The raven's trinkets held magic in them. She'd left it on the window sill for him to find when he'd gone back to the house with Mom. It was the raven's way of telling him she was sorry for his loss, though how a young crow understood so much was beyond him.

Maybe she'd been his spirit animal.

If he hadn't held her gift in his hand now, he could've convinced himself she hadn't existed at all.

EIGHT

Maybe this was what a panic attack felt like. Aviana gripped the wheel and tried to stop panting. Keep it up, and she was going to pass out.

Shit, she couldn't do this.

She thought of Easton's kiss last night and shook her head to rattle out the weak thoughts. Yes, she could, because Easton had been gentle with her. He wasn't all weapons and darkness. He was good in his middle, just like he always had been.

Last night, she'd seen the spark of the boy she'd fallen in love with.

Easton was hers.

By the time she pulled under the Grayland Mobile Park sign, however, she was back to full-blown panic-mode. Today, she was going to put herself out there further than she ever had in her entire life. She was going to declare what she needed to make her life into the one she wanted.

Unfortunately, that life had somehow grown to include a crew of bear shifters—her biggest natural fear. From early childhood, she'd been told how volatile and murderous the apex predator shifters were. They weren't like her people, who were scavenger shifters, politely preying on already deceased things. Bears killed what they wanted and didn't give second thoughts to carcasses.

Great risk brought the possibility of great reward, though, and Easton was worth it. He really was. *Deep breath. Chest out, back straight. Smile. Bigger. Let's do this.*

The Gray Backs sat around a communal fire pit in front of a semi-circle of trailers. They wore light jackets to ward off the cool March night and sat in brightly-colored plastic chairs. Easton wasn't here. Well, good. This would be easier without him watching because she wasn't here to see Easton right now. She was here to talk to his alpha, Creed.

The Gray Backs had gone quiet by the time she stumbled out of her car. "Hi!" she said, much more high pitched than she'd intended as she flapped her hand in a wave.

"Ha! Pay up, Griz," Willa said, pointing to Matt.

Matt rolled his eyes and handed Willa a wadded up five dollar bill from his pocket.

Okaay.

A yipping attack dog the size of a soccer ball charged Aviana and bounced around her feet, barking. It was brown and white, and someone has shaved a mohawk down the entire length of his back and head. She would've been more intimidated if he didn't lick her ankles between barks.

"Peanut Butter Spike. Get down!" Gia commanded.

Aviana stepped gingerly around the yapper and opened the back door, then struggled under the weight of a massive box of beer cans. She hefted it toward the Gray Backs, breathing heavily as she stumbled forward, trying not to step on the tiny dog circling her feet. She set the gift on the ledge of the brick fire pit. "I did research on lumberjacks, and the Internet said you were hairy, wore flannel, belched a lot, and drank lots of beer."

Willa grabbed her stomach and cackled. "What site were you looking on?"

"The first one that came up on the results." Good God, she wished she could lift her gaze from the ground right now. "Anyway, I brought you this." She pushed the box forward, but it only moved by an inch. Silly, weak bird arms. Peanut Butter Spike probably could've moved it more.

"I like her," Jason said, ripping into the side and pulling a blue can out.

"How did you find out where we live?" Creed asked, his eyes narrowed in suspicion.

"Oh. Uuuh, it said it on Jason's social media pages." Had it? She couldn't remember. She'd known they lived here because she flew over it every day, but they didn't need to know that she was a quiet observer to their lives.

"Dude," Matt said, leveling Jason with a glare.

"Like you can talk! You were the king of oversharing before you deleted all your pages. Piss off, man. It's not like I ever thought anyone would be able to actually find the trailer park. We're out in the wilderness. I assumed GPS would laugh at anyone who tried to get up the back roads in these mountains."

Creed was glaring at him with a tired, not amused expression.

Jason shrugged. "Fine. I'll take any mention of our address off my pages."

Creed swung his attention to Aviana, who

was feeling mighty guilty for outing Jason to save herself right about now. "What are you doing here?"

Aviana lifted her chin and tried to hold his gaze, but failed. Fuck it all, just spit it out then. "I'm here to ask you for Easton."

Jason choked on his beer and spewed it into a fine mist in the air.

"What do you mean, ask for Easton?" Creed asked over the coughing.

She inhaled deeply and said, "I'm here to ask your permission to court Easton."

"Explain."

Aviana held onto the side of the waist-high, bricked-in fire pit to steady her wobbly legs and swallowed hard. "I want to date him with the intention of becoming his mate."

"That's not how we do things here. Mates are chosen freely." Creed looked her up and down as his nostrils flared. "You smell like terror. I know Easton. I don't think you are it for him. He isn't made for a mate. I'm sorry, but the answer is no."

"Aw, piss off, Creed," Willa muttered. She pitched her voice up and yelled, "Beaston!"

"Willa," Creed warned.

"As Second, I veto your bullshittery. She likes him, she brought us beer, and she won me five fuckin' dollars." Willa cocked her head and her eyebrows jacked up. "Winner, winner, werebear dinner."

"Second, Willa. *Second*. Not alpha. I'm alpha, and I say she isn't going to be safe around Easton. I'm all for Easton finding someone, but she's human, and he's...well...Beaston."

"He hasn't killed Gia yet," Willa argued, pointing to Creed's mate.

Creed looked at Gia in disbelief. "I'm not the bad guy in this. I'm trying to save her life."

"He won't hurt me," Aviana murmured. She would ignore the slice under her arm that was just now scabbing over.

"Baby," Gia said rubbing Creed's arm. "I know you mean well, but Aviana is asking your permission to court him out of respect. It's not really up to you." She nodded to the man limping toward them from the tree line. "It's up to him."

Creed scrubbed his hands down his face and muttered, "Fuck."

As he approached, Easton's eyes reflected eerily in the glow from the fire in the brick pit—proof that his animal was never far from the surface. His gray shirt clung to his hard physique, and the top two buttons were open, exposing the line between his pec muscles. His legs were long and powerful with every stride he took, and despite the limp, he was graceful. He'd learned that gate with his time in the wilderness, fending for himself. She'd watched the slow change from clumsy boy to graceful animal in the years that broke him.

"Hi," she whispered past her tightening vocal cords.

He shifted his weight from foot to foot, just on the edge of the firelight. Even in his human form, he looked like a wild animal who found safety in the shadows. "You're here."

"For a reason," Willa said.

Easton frowned and ghosted a glance at the red-headed woman, then back to Aviana. "Why?"

Aviana looked to Creed. He was king here, and she was wary of him snapping if she didn't behave right.

"Go ahead," the alpha said in a defeated tone, leaning back in his chair and resting his hand on the swell of his mate's stomach.

"I want to court you."

Easton shrugged a shoulder up to his ear and shook his head. "I don't know what that means."

"I want to date you, and if you find you like

me well enough..." She swallowed the lump in her throat, but the rest of the words wouldn't come out. Not with him staring at her so directly like this.

"If I like you well enough...what?"

"Maybe don't look at me while I tell you."

"All right," he said, sounding baffled. He turned around and gave her his back.

She exhaled a long, shaky breath. "Maybe if you like me well enough, you'll pick me for a mate."

Easton's back went rigid. With each silent second that dragged on, the anticipation clogged her throat, making it harder and harder to breathe. She opened her mouth to apologize for intruding and excuse herself, but Easton murmured, "You're scared of me."

"I'll work on not being scared of you."

"Then okay."

"Okay?" Her voice came out a hopeful squeak.

"Easton, I forbid you to Turn her," Creed said, powerful voice sending electric currents into the air.

Easton looked to Willa over his shoulder and shook his head. "I learned my lesson. I won't Turn Ana." He spun slowly on his heel and looked at Aviana over the firelight. "I won't be any good at this." There was warning in his tone, but his eyes softened. "But we can try. Alpha, I want your blessing." He turned his inhuman, green gaze on Creed. "Please."

A muscle twitched in Creed's clenched jaw. With a sigh, he leveled Aviana with a glare. "Before you answer the question I'm about to ask you, know that we can all hear a lie."

Steeling herself, Aviana nodded.

"Why do you want to be with Easton?"

That question held the easiest answer in the world. "Because I don't fit anywhere else."

Softly, Willa murmured, "She sounds like a Gray Back to me."

A slow smile spread across Creed's face in the flickering firelight. "Then a courtship between you and Easton has my blessing."

A giggle bubbled up her throat, and she sagged heavily against the brick as Easton stood frozen across the fire, looking stunned. Willa stood and reached her first, then hugged her so hard her lungs hurt. Gia and Georgia followed, and the boys smiled and nodded at her as she walked around the fire pit toward Easton—her Easton.

"I won't hurt you," he said, promise in his voice.

She stood on her tiptoes and hugged his

neck, inhaling the wild scent of his skin. Fur and earth and pine. "I know you won't. I trust you."

His hands slipped around her waist slowly, gently, as if he were forcing himself to be careful with her. "When you get to know me, you'll leave."

She eased back and smiled up at him, trying her best to hold his feral gaze. She pressed her palm against his chest. Her hand rattled with the soft vibration of his pounding heart. "I already know you."

Confusion rippled over his face like a wave, there and gone in a moment. "Do you want to see my den?"

"I want to see your den," Jason piped up.

"No," Easton gritted out.

"How do you like that?" he asked Georgia. "I'm his best friend, and he still won't let me see the inside of his trailer."

"Nobody's seen it," Matt said. "Hey!" he called as Aviana and Easton walked toward the tree line. "I'll give you five bucks to tell us what it looks like inside."

Aviana shook her head and ignored the banter that kicked up near the fire pit. "Don't worry," she said softly. "I won't tell anyone anything you don't want me to."

Easton didn't say anything back, only slipped his big, strong, calloused hand around hers and squeezed gently. That was a reward in itself, so she bumped his shoulder and snuggled her cheek against his taut arm. A sign of devotion from a raven, but he didn't need to know about her animal side. Not yet. Not until she figured out a way to break it to him gently. Easton refusing to share his home with his crew was proof he was a keeper of secrets. Her instincts said he would be upset if he knew she'd witnessed the years that had shattered him. No, before she exposed her hidden feathered self, she had to make sure he wouldn't run away from what they could be.

By the time they'd walked up the trail to his singlewide—the one with the chipped white siding and stacks of firewood down one whole side—she wasn't shaking so badly anymore. She did, however, feel as if she'd been dumped into a surreal moment that could very well be a dream. She was here, with *him*. With the one she'd thought so much about and forsaken her people for. With the one who'd kept her trinkets after all these years.

"I'm sorry," he murmured as he pushed his door open, though she couldn't tell what he was apologizing for.

She stepped up the stairs and into his den as he flipped the light switch on. The smell of pine sap hit her senses first as she took in the small space of the living room. There was only one lamp in the corner, and he'd thrown a square of orange fabric over it to mute the light. The walls were covered from floor to ceiling with tree bark. She gasped as it hit her why this place felt so familiar. She spun and stuck her head back out the front door, but she already knew what she would find. A workshop built at a similar distance from the tree Easton had built a house in when he was a cub. This place was his version of the home he'd lived in all those years ago. He'd recreated the place he felt the safest.

A wash of mixed emotions filled her. Sadness that those years had etched their way so deeply into his adult life. Disappointment that he was still holding onto the past. Pride that he'd survived at all. Tears blurred her vision as she smiled up at him. He was waiting, dark eyebrows furrowed with worry.

"I love it," she whispered thickly.

The tension melted from his shoulders, and he huffed a relieved sigh. A crooked smile took his lips, almost deep enough to expose one of his dimples, but not quite.

He showed her the small kitchen and single bedroom, which took up half the length of the trailer and was curiously normal after the tree-like living room. A queen-size bed boasted crisp white sheets under a folded down comforter that looked as soft as a cloud. His bathroom was just as tidy—a habit he must've picked up in his adult years because the boy she remembered had been scattered and his living space cluttered.

She brushed her fingers across the plush comforter, familiarizing herself with his place. There was a bookshelf along the wall three shelves high and made of oak. The top shelf was filled with childbirth books. She pulled one out and looked questioningly at him.

"Creed got Gia with a baby." With a frown, he sat on the bed behind her. "My mom didn't survive a baby. I wanted to make sure Gia would be okay."

Aviana's heart dropped to the floor. Of course he would be worried after what happened.

Easton's mouth ticked as he pulled at the edges of the frayed black ribbon she'd gifted him the night his father died. She swallowed the gasp and froze into place so she wouldn't attract his attention before she could get the shock wiped off her face. Where had he pulled that from?

"I like Gia. I was mad at Creed for putting her at risk, but she loves her baby. She wants it. Even though Gia is human, she isn't weak. And her baby girl is strong, too." He lifted his gaze to hers. "She'll be dragon-blooded, you know."

"Dragon-blooded?" Aviana asked, leaning back against the dresser. That sounded terrifying.

"Creed is the grandson of the last immortal dragon. He turned out grizzly, and maybe his daughter will, too. Or maybe not. Gia promised to have the baby in a hospital. Registered shifters can do that now. It's not like when I was growing up, and we had to hide our young."

She knew all about that. It had been the same for raven shifters. Until they were old enough to control their Changes, it was safest to live away from society, off the grid somewhere. It was still like that for growing families. Ravens weren't out to the public like other shifters and likely never would be. Ravens were naturally more cautious than bears.

"I'm sorry about your mom." Her voice quivered with emotion. Oh, how she'd wanted to say those words to him, but she'd only been able to bring him gifts and hope he interpreted her sympathy.

He pulled the black ribbon through his fingers and gave her that ghost of a smile. "Don't be. It was a long time ago. I was a cub at the time. I barely even remember what she looks like." His voice sounded odd though—hollow—and she'd bet her flight feathers he remembered everything in great detail. His mind had always been like that. Sharp as a blade, retaining everything he learned. It's how he'd survived out there in those harsh woods alone at such a young age. He would try something until he figured out how it worked, and then he never made the same mistakes twice. His mind was a steel trap, just like the one—

Aviana closed her eyes against the vision of Easton screaming. Not now. Later, when she was alone. She couldn't feed that memory now while he watched her with those bright eyes that missed nothing.

"You're hungry." Easton stood so fast he blurred, and she gasped at his speed.

Easton held his hands out. "Sorry," he

whispered.

"I think you're being gentle around me."

He nodded.

"Is it in your nature to be gentle?"

He shook his head slowly.

"Then I think maybe you should be yourself and allow me to adjust."

"But you always smell scared. I don't like it."

"If I get used to you, then I won't be such a chicken anymore, and I have a feeling I'll like your real self even better, anyway."

His eyebrows jacked up. "I assure you, you won't."

Aviana snorted and laughed. "How do you know?"

His eyes dipped to her lips as they stretched into a bigger smile. "Because I'm pretty damned sure no one on this planet can handle all of my...personality." But now a smile was spreading across his face, and there they were—those dimples she'd wished with all of her heart to see.

Before she could change her mind, she stepped forward and pressed her finger against one. She'd seen them a hundred times in his youth but had never revealed herself as a human, and couldn't touch the tiny indentations as a bird.

He inhaled a sharp breath as his pupils contracted to pinpoints and zeroed in on her. "What are you doing?"

"I like to touch you. And I like when you smile big enough for me to see these." She moved out of the way of a dresser and looked at his reflection in the mirror with him. "Your smile is my favorite thing about you."

"Are you broken, Ana?"

The question caught her off guard, and she had to wait a moment before answering, just to steady her thoughts. "Not broken, no."

"Then why did you ask for me? Why did you come to my alpha for me? Why in the hell would you want to be mated to a man like me?"

"Because my life doesn't feel hollow when I'm around you," she said honestly.

He huffed a humorless laugh and looked down at the ribbon between his fingertips. "You make no sense."

"I wasn't happy—"

"Happy is just a word, Ana. It doesn't really exist. It's a state of mind people convince themselves they have so they can get through their existence one day at a time. You search for happiness, and when you think you find it, you work your whole life to hang onto this feeling as thin as air, and then you die. *Happy* is a bullshit word."

Shocked, she sank down to the bed beside him. She'd never heard him string so many words together. He'd never been vocal about his opinions when he was younger, and now it was clear how jaded he'd become. He was wrong, though.

"Well then, I'll make you happy and prove you wrong." She stuck her tongue out at him and grinned.

Easton cocked his head and stared at her smile again. It seemed to attract his attention easily. "Whatever your reasons," he murmured, "I'm glad you found me."

NINE

Easton's focus was dragged to Ana's lips for the hundredth time. She smiled the more comfortable around him she became. She didn't smell like fear anymore. Just vanilla.

What was it about her lips? Right now, she was sitting beside him on the living room couch, talking about her first job. She'd waited tables at some diner where she lived, and she had lots of funny stories about the people she'd worked with. Her lips looked like art as they formed each word.

Or maybe it was the kiss from last night he kept thinking about. The feel of her lips against his. He'd never once had the urge to kiss the other girls in the Gray Backs, but around Ana, it was all he could think about. *Focus. She's looking. She'll think you're weird like everyone else does. Keep her.*

"So, what do you do for fun?"

"What do you do?" he countered. Not because he was avoiding the question, but because he was suddenly excruciatingly curious about what filled up her quiet hours.

Ana scrunched up her nose. "Don't laugh."

"I won't."

"Pinky promise." She lifted her pinky in the air. "Hook your pinky onto mine and say, I pinky promise not to laugh."

He did as she asked and reveled in the feel of her. So much so that he didn't let go of her finger after he recited the oath. He just sank farther back into the couch cushion beside her with their pinkies hooked. She put her legs over his lap as if they'd known each other for always. He smiled at how fucking cute she was.

"I like to knit."

"Like old ladies do? Hats and socks and blankets?"

"No. You're smiling, Easton. Don't let that get out of hand." She waited for him to wipe his amusement off his face before she continued. "I knit clothes for animals. Turtle sweaters with spikes on the back, and dog costumes for Halloween. I even made a dress for a guinea pig wedding once. People send me special requests online, and I make them."

Easton waited for the laugh to die in his throat before he asked, "And they pay you money for these…costumes?"

Ana lifted her chin proudly. "Yes. I never told Caden about that stuff because I knew he would think it stupid and beneath me, and he would ask me to give it up."

"Caden was your last mate?" His bear rattled a long growl inside of him.

Ana let go of his pinky and pressed her palm against his chest. "Not my choice. He was a smart pairing, but I didn't care for him."

"I would like to see a dress for a guinea pig."

Ana dropped her gaze to her hand, but it didn't hide her smile. Maybe happiness did exist. Ana looked happy now.

"Now, your turn. Tell me what you like to do."

No one had ever asked him this before, so he took his time answering. "I like to chop wood."

"Why?"

"Because it makes me feel like my bear isn't going to rip out of my skin."

The smile fell from Ana's face. "Does it feel like that often?"

He nodded. Best she know what she was in for. "All the time."

"Every minute?"

He nodded. "Except it's not so bad when I'm around you. Or chopping firewood."

"What do you do with the wood?"

"I could take care of you."

She propped a pair of throw pillows under her head and relaxed against the couch, her legs still draped over him. She was wearing jean shorts, so he rested his hand on her smooth legs. "Did you shave your legs?" he asked.

"Mmm hmm."

"Did you shave my legs for me? In case I touched you here?" When he ran his fingertip up her shin, she shivered.

"Yes," she said on a breath. Her face had gone all serious, and her pupils dilated, making the blue in her eyes look darker. "Now stop distracting me. What did you mean about taking care of me? I don't want money, Easton. I just want you."

"A cord of lumber goes for two-hundred fifty to three-hundred dollars come wintertime around here. I chop all spring and summer and sell in the fall after the first snow."

"Sell to who?"

"Until Jason came along, I sold to backwoodsman. People who didn't care I was a little...off. People who needed firewood because they hadn't chopped enough for themselves because they were too old or sick or they couldn't find enough dead trees. They have to be dead a long time so the heavy green middles dry out and turn white. Those are the ones that burn the best. I can charge more if I split it for them and deliver it to their cabins."

"I thought you worked up in the mountains as a lumberjack."

"That's one of my jobs. I have three. My animal does best if I stay busy. He's still wild as shit, but a busy mind makes him manageable. Kind of."

"Jason helps you now?"

"He's my friend. We went in as partners this past fall. I had a lot of wood to unload, we needed to sell closer to town, and I can't talk to people. I can't. Jason's good. He talks. I chop."

"I like Jason. It's a good business you two are doing."

He stroked his finger up and down her leg, watching the chills that washed up her soft skin in waves. "Logging is seasonal, so we all work different jobs during fire-season."

"What else do you like to do?"

"Kiss you." He tossed her a sideways glance and slid out from under her legs. If he kissed her here in his den where she was spreading around her sexy scent—pheromones and vanilla—he would want more. Ana was fragile. Ana couldn't bed a man like him. Easton stood and held out his hand, palm up. "Do you want to see what else I like to do?"

Her lips parted slightly, and she blinked slowly as she slid her palm against his and nodded. He liked that he had such an effect on her. She smelled so fucking good he wanted to bury his face between her legs, but he wouldn't. He liked Ana. He wanted to keep her, not scare her.

She was wearing a thin, soft, black blouse, and the gooseflesh he'd conjured so easily on her legs bothered him, so he pulled his heavy canvas jacket off the coat rack by the front door. He draped it over her shoulders before he led her out the front door. It was lined with wool and would keep her warm.

He gave a private smile when he heard her sniff the jacket. Little human knew how to use some of her senses at least.

"Easton?" Ana asked. Her voice sounded odd as she tugged his hand. The porch light illuminated her troubled eyes, so he drew up closer. Perhaps she was still cold. Or hungry or thirsty or tired or sick. She didn't smell sick. He didn't really know how to take care of humans.

"I want to tell you something." Ana searched his eyes as she snuggled deeper into his jacket.

"Okay." This sounded bad. He was always ready for bad, though.

She didn't answer for a long time. Instead, some of the fear smell came back, and she couldn't hold his gaze anymore. At last, she smiled faintly and whispered, "Thank you for the jacket."

That wasn't what she'd meant to say. It wouldn't have been so hard for her to thank him. He forgot manners all the time, but Ana wasn't like him. She was socialized. Or civilized. But there were a million things he wasn't ready to tell her, too, so he wouldn't push. That wouldn't be fair. "It's okay if you have secrets."

Her big blue eyes were rimming with tears. She nodded slowly as her chin quivered from where she was trying to keep her emotions bottled up.

"Soft and full of tears," he murmured as he thumbed away the first drop that fell from her eye to her cheek.

"Do you have secrets, Easton?"

"Infinite secrets." More secrets than stars in the sky.

"If you ever want to tell me, I'll help you keep them."

Easton made a ticking sound behind his teeth and eased away from her. Danger. Scritch scratch. Secrets and memories were the same. They belonged to the dark. He was strong enough to hold them, but Ana was too fragile to shoulder his broken pieces. He would spare her the pain because he liked her. He was the avalanche, and she the hummingbird, and the only real gift he could give her was to not crash down upon her and crush her into oblivion.

"Come," he murmured, pulling her toward his workshop. This place was as sacred as his den, but he wanted to share everything with Ana. It was as much of himself as he could show her. "Wait here." He didn't want her tripping over the workbench in the middle or any of his tools he might have left lying about. When he pulled the string to the single lightbulb that hung from the ceiling, it illuminated the entire shop. Easy to do since it wasn't very big. He could've built it much bigger, but this was the size of the workshop Dad had used. In a shop just this size, Easton had learned to be a knife maker.

He watched with a ready smile as her eyes drifted over the tools hung on the wall and the workbench with the trio of wooden handles held together with clamps, ready for staining. She looked at the bowl of discarded blades he kept telling himself he would salvage someday because steel like that deserved a home in a fine leather sheath. He would right his mistakes: bad cuts and notches, weak spots in the steel, and experimental decorative edges gone wrong.

She padded over the sawdust floor and touched the finished hilt of a knife that was ready for a sheath. "Easton," she whispered. "These are beautiful."

Sure, he knew they were fine knives, but hearing Ana compliment his work filled him with pride. Slowly, so he wouldn't startle her, he squared up behind her and reached around her. Gently, he took the knife from her hands and set it on the table. Brushing his lips against her neck just to taste the skin there, he picked up the sharp awl he used for engraving.

E + A, he carved neatly into the hilt. Girls liked things that matched, and now she would have one just like Willa, Gia, and Georgia. "This is yours. My first gift to you." The first of many if he didn't scare her away.

Ana sniffled and leaned back against him. She nuzzled her cheek against his once. Affectionate little creature. She liked to do that. Soft skin against his raspy whiskers. He smiled and slid the knife into one of the sheaths that had been hanging up to dry. The *snap* of the button clasp was loud in the silence of his workshop, but now it was safe for her to handle with the razor-sharp blade tucked away.

Ana turned in his arms, and her eyes swam with such adoration it nearly buckled his knees. No one had ever looked at him like this. Like he was everything.

"I'm going to kiss you," he warned.

She slipped her arms around his neck and leaned up. "Good."

He tried to stay gentle, he really did, but when Ana bit his lip and gripped the back of his hair, he lost control over his animal fast. He lifted her onto the workbench and dug his fingers into her hips in desperation to keep himself in check. A growl rattled his throat as she nipped him again. "Careful, woman."

A whiff of fear, and then nothing but arousal again, and it was plain as day Ana was finding her bravery with him. He smiled against her lips and plunged his tongue into her mouth. He dragged her forward across the table until her legs wrapped around him and her sex pressed against his raging erection. With a soft moan, Ana rolled her hips against his, and he just about lost it. Heaving breath, he trailed kisses down her neck to try and steady himself. His eyes would scare her if she saw them right now, so when she tried to pull his gaze to hers, he closed his eyes and angled his face away from her.

"What's wrong?" she asked, hugging him tightly.

"I want you," he gritted out. Wanted to be buried inside of her, but she deserved better.

"You can have me. I've waited so long for this." She rested her palm on his cheek and pulled his gaze back to hers again. Honesty pooled in her deep blue eyes when she whispered, "I'm yours."

"Won't risk putting a baby in you."

"You can't. I'm on the pill."

Easton grazed her shoulder with his teeth,

then kissed it gently. "I don't know what that means."

"I'm on medicine that means you can't get me pregnant."

Well shit, that was sorcery right there. "It's too soon."

Ana huffed a mysterious laugh. "It's really *really* not."

"You're fragile, and I'll hurt you." Why the fuck was he arguing?

One of Ana's delicate eyebrows arched high. "You won't impale me, Easton. Just make love to me gently."

"Gently," he repeated. That word sounded impossible right now. "Gentle won't work in here. If I take you on my work bench, I'll fuck you like a rutting animal." He pulled her off the table and whipped her around, then strode toward his trailer with her legs still wrapped around his waist. White sheets. Clean bed. His Ana deserved slow and comfortable and easy.

Ana sucked on his neck hard as he carried her through the front door and into his bedroom. Shit she felt so good against him like this. Lowering her back onto the bed, he kissed her lips and rocked his hips against hers. She bowed against the mattress. So sensitive to him. It made this easier. No hesitation. No questions. Everything was natural with her.

Easton lifted off her just enough to pull his shirt over his head. He ducked in to kiss her again, but she said, "Whoa, whoa, whoa, whoa, mister." Her eyes went wide as she studied his torso. He looked down at himself, but nothing was amiss. He didn't have scars like Matt or anything unsightly.

"What's wrong?"

"You just…" Ana looked stunned as she gave a slow-motion blink and shook her head. "You just grew up right."

"You make no sense."

But as her palms drifted over his collar bones, down the curve of his pecs and over the ridges of his abs, he understood. She liked the way he looked. Her fingers shook as she unhooked the button of his jeans. Easton grabbed her hand to steady the tremble there. "Are you nervous?"

"A little. You?"

He should be, but he wasn't. He'd never been surer of anything before. "No."

She swallowed audibly and unzipped his pants. Then with her fingers inside his briefs, she pushed the remainder of his clothes down his hips. His dick hit air but wasn't lonely for long. Ana pulled a gentle stroke with her warm hand that conjured a satisfied feral noise from his throat. Arms locked on either side of her head, he rolled his hips with her next pull. Shit he was too sensitive to her. Another minute of this, and he'd cream her shirt. Shirt, shirt, shirt—why was she still wearing a shirt? Straddling her, he pulled her top over her head and marveled at the black lace contraption that was pushing her perky boobs up to her collar bones. Floored, he ripped into her jeans and pulled them down to expose the matching see-through panties.

"Did you wear these for me?"

Ana smiled shyly and nodded. Holy fuck, she was gorgeous. Black lace and blushing cheeks. He could see between her legs. Tiny peeks through the lace. She'd shaved there too. He needed inside of her. Now.

With a growl, he pulled her panties down and flung them to the floor, then pulled off the tit holder she'd just unsnapped. Oooh, her nipples were perfect. Pink like her cheeks and all drawn up against the cold. He should warm them with his mouth. Leaning forward, he drew one in and sucked on it. When she responded with a helpless sound, he ran the flat of his tongue over it and cupped his hand over her sex. Her body moved against him like water. Every touch ushered a reaction. His dick was so hard right now. Too thick. Looking at Ana, this couldn't work. She was tiny, fine boned like a bird. He would hurt her.

But when he brushed her folds with his middle finger, she was soaking wet. Damn, he wanted to taste her there. Wanted to taste? Was that normal? *Don't scare her.*

Ana reached down and pressed his hand against her harder as she writhed against his touch. "In," she pleaded.

In? A little more pressure, and his finger slid into her by inches. Ana threw back her head as her eyes rolled closed. Oh fuck, that hole wasn't only for dicks. His finger felt good to her, too. He eased inside of her up to his knuckle, but that wasn't what got her going. When he bumped the spot right above her entrance, Ana cried out and clutched the comforter. Her knees spread wider, as if she was inviting him in again.

That was the spot she liked. That was the spot he needed to work. So he did.

"Stop, stop, stop," she whispered. "I'm going to come."

Easton slid out of her immediately. Wasn't coming what she wanted?

"I want to come with you."

Oh. Easton kissed her hard as he lay down on top of her. Ana's breasts were soft against his hard chest—more opposites. He positioned the head of his cock at her slick entrance and teased. Ana begged by rolling her hips until she took him an inch, then again. How could anything feel this good?

"Please," she pleaded. "I want you inside of me."

Gritting his teeth against the intense pleasure, Easton slid into her tight entrance until she'd taken all of him. He eased out slowly as she clutched onto his back with her claws. Scratching little mate. *Mate, mate, mate.* Easton pumped his hips hard once, then eased out again, savoring her body. Ana begged him to go faster, but he wouldn't. He wasn't after a thirty second fuck-fest with her. He wanted to take care of her before he shot his load.

He kissed her to quiet her pleading, brushed his tongue against hers over and over until she gripped the back of his hair and pulled him even closer. Hard in, easy out. Hard in, easy out.

"Easton, please!" Ana cried, arching her neck back.

"Fuck," he growled out, bucking into her

faster.

Over and over he slammed into her as the pressure built in his dick. Ana ran her claws down his back and screamed out his name as her body pulsed around him, milking him.

His mind was going, filling with the snarling, possessive monster inside of him. *No, no, no, hold on!* Growling out a wild sound, he lost his mind and drove into her one last time. Heat flooded out of him in throbbing spurts.

My mate. Mine.

He wanted to keep his Ana for always.

And as he bucked erratically into her, emptying himself completely, he did the unforgivable.

He sank his teeth deep into her shoulder.

TEN

Aviana cried out at the mixture of pleasure and poignant pain that shot jolts of electricity firing down the nerves of her shoulder and arm. She gasped as Easton clamped his teeth down harder. He went rigid above her and released her torn skin, then flinched away from her. In a blur, he was in the shadows against the wall, light reflecting oddly in his eyes.

The scent of iron filled the air, and warmth ran rivers down her shoulder and onto the sheets. She clutched her shoulder as tears of agony ran down the corners of her eyes. Why had he done that?

"Easton, you hurt me," she murmured in a broken voice. "Why?"

"Ana, Ana, I'm sorry. Fuck." He jumped up on the bed, legs on either side of hers as he held out his hands to calm her. His eyes glowed in the light that filtered in from the bathroom. He really was an animal. Wild and violent, and not even her affection could slow his destruction.

"I love you Easton, and you hurt me!" Anger blasted through her. Betrayal lashed against her heart.

"Don't say that, Ana! You don't love me. Can't love me. You don't know me." Easton dragged his horrified gaze across her hand that had gone slick with blood. It wasn't stopping. Putting pressure on it wasn't working. "Ana, Ana, listen. You're going to Turn. I put a bear inside of you. I'm sorry, Ana!" He fell to his knees, straddling her hips. "I'm so sorry. My bear— No! I did it. It's my responsibility. I have to get you help. Creed will know what to do. I messed everything up. I'm so sorry."

Aviana searched Easton's eyes. This made no sense. Why had he bitten her? To Turn her? Creed had forbidden it. "What will Creed do if he finds out?"

"Any minute now, any minute now. Your first Change shouldn't be with the monster who broke you." Easton lifted her in his arms like she weighed nothing at all and strode through the house. He yanked open the front door as she clutched her shoulder, but he hadn't answered her question.

"Easton! What will Creed do?"

"Kill me, as I deserve."

"Oh, Easton, what have you done?"

Creed wouldn't find a bear in her, though. There wasn't room for one. A raven had claimed her since birth. Easton didn't know it, but he never had a chance of Turning her into a bear. "Stop," she whispered as he blasted past the woodpile. "Easton, stop. I have to tell you something."

Confusion and regret marred his features as he set her down. His eyes were bright and resigned, and his body had gone rigid. He wasn't going to hide her injury. He was marching to his death to find her help. She couldn't let him do that.

"You didn't Turn me," she murmured, searching for the right words that would fix this. "I told you to be yourself with me, and you were. I was surprised, but it's okay. The bite is okay. We both got lost in the moment."

"What do you mean I didn't Turn you?" Easton's eyes drifted to her arm, the opposite one he'd bitten, and back to her face. He canted his head and frowned, then looked at her arm again. The healing slice under her arm was what was drawing his attention. He took a step back and angled his face away from her, eyes never straying from hers. "What's on your arm, Ana?"

"A cut."

"From what?" Easton's voice came out a low rumbling growl, more animal than human.

She exhaled slowly, shakily, then whispered, "Someone threw a knife at me."

"Who?"

She closed her eyes, and twin tears escaped down her cheeks.

"Who, Ana?" he yelled, frightening the birds roosting in the trees around them into the air and making her jump.

"You."

Easton paced, hands linked behind his head as he shook it. "Show me."

"Show you what?"

"Show me my raven! Show me what betrayal looks like. Feathers, feathers, show me your feathers. I suffered out there alone! All those years. Years and years. Show me the bird who watched me break and then *left me*." Agony filled Easton's eyes as he leaned against the woodpile and slammed his head back. "Please, Ana. Do it fast."

Aviana's shoulders shook with sobs of

agony. She hadn't known he saw her that way. She'd tried to help, not hurt him worse. Closing her eyes, she let the raven have her body. The Change was instant, and she beat her powerful wings against the pain in her shoulder. Harder she pressed against the air currents until she sat on the lowest branch of the closest pine, staring at the man who owned her heart. At the man who was looking at her with such heartbreak in his eyes. Chin at his chest, he whispered, "You can't love me, raven. You don't know how." Easton stepped forward and yelled. His yell turned to a roar that shook the trees, and a giant, silver grizzly burst from his skin.

He could've reached her from here, as big as he was. He could've charged and ripped her from the branch, but Easton did something much worse instead. He lifted those glowing green eyes to her and exposed his crippling sadness. Her heart burned, as if he had reached into her chest cavity and yanked it out between her ribs.

He turned his back on her and walked away through the trees, moonlight shining off his gray back.

And just like that, Easton—her Easton—was gone.

ELEVEN

Easton buttoned the fly of the too big jeans he'd snatched from a laundry line of a cabin fifteen miles back. He didn't mind nudity, but here, it was different. Here, a layer of protection felt necessary.

With a steadying breath, he scanned the clearing where he'd grown up. It had taken him all night and part of the day to travel here as a bear, and now the sun sat high in the morning sky, casting the rubble of his childhood home in light.

The yard was overgrown, and young saplings had sprung up here and there. The wild grass had recovered from the winter and already came up to his thighs. He ran his hands over the top of the waving grass as he approached the charred rubble of the house he'd grown up in. The faint scent of smoke still clung to the burned lumber after all these years. Only the porch stairs remained intact, and moss and vibrant green overgrowth had blanketed all but the seared ends of the wood. This had been where he had burned Mom and all of her belongings, just like she'd asked.

Easton's lip twitched at the residual anger he had for her. She hadn't even tried. He couldn't begin to imagine where her head had been when she'd gone into labor. It hadn't been on him or the baby. Maybe she had gone mad with grief, or maybe she had already accepted her fate from that dream she kept raging about as her fever spiked. It had taken her two days to die, and all the while, Easton had done everything an eight-year-old boy could to save her and the baby.

He'd seen awful things in this house.

Easton slammed the door and pressed his frail shoulder blades against it, then slid down the splintered length of it, sobbing. The baby had stopped moving yesterday, and now Mom was gone, too. It wasn't fair.

He screamed his rage into the abyss as something shifted inside of him. Fear, anger, loss...loneliness. There would be no more room for happiness. The world was ugly, and now it would swallow him up. No matter. His insides were ugly now, too.

"Shit," Easton rasped out, sinking down onto the creaking porch stair.

Everything had gotten so messed up here. His entire life had been shaped in the three-day window when he'd lost his family.

He'd dragged the supplies they'd gathered for winter from the house into the shed. Even at eight, he'd known it was an awful idea to burn his shelter, but it was that or go back into that room with Mom's body. No, Dad had gotten a funeral pyre in the clearing. Mom got the cabin.

The raven brought him two more black ribbons. One for Mom and one for the baby. He'd knotted those together and kept them in his pocket to stop his weak tears when the hurt welled up too deeply. He'd set out on his own, headed due north the next day to find help, only to get lost and turned around, and to come back three days later dehydrated, hungry, and feeling even more empty than he had before. That first winter he'd lived in Dad's workshop. Easton had rationed the supplies they'd gathered and insulated the outside of the shed with spruce limbs and mud shoved in the cracks, but it was still so bone-deep cold he'd almost died of it. He came out of that first season emaciated and heartbroken. And the raven was waiting. Always waiting on the bottom branches of a lodgepole pine. He couldn't control his shifts very well anymore. Sometime in those lonely months, his bear had decided he was better off without those pesky human emotions, and he'd begun to take over. Easton hadn't minded so much back then. He wouldn't have survived without his animal instincts driving him to carve a life out of that harsh wilderness. He hadn't known it at the time, but giving his bear that much power cost him his soul.

The raven had saved his sanity when he was a cub trying to figure out how to fend for himself, but just barely.

Every year got harder, and that young crow had been there, always watching, leaving him trinkets to find right when he needed a pick-me-up, as if she could see him wearing down. He should've known she was more than what she seemed, but she'd been there as long as he could remember, and to him, she was an intelligent animal who had become his friend. She'd ridden his hump when he'd gotten older and his muscle mass had started coming in. She'd sat on top of him, tiny talons clutching his fur as she rocked back and forth with his lumbering gate—content to just be. When he'd caught his first fish in the stream near the clearing, he'd tossed her a scrap because that's what friends did. They shared.

Easton stood and sauntered over to the shed his Dad had built. It was still standing but was leaning dangerously to the side. The weather had gotten to it and rotted most of the wood. Inside, old rusted blades and tools were scattered about. Small animals had made several burrows inside, probably in the wintertime to keep from freezing. On the back wall, on an old, rust-colored nail, still hung the snares he'd made.

The raven had brought him one that first spring after his family had passed. He was starving and wasn't hunting with any success, and the vegetable garden, the first he'd planted by himself, hadn't been producing much. He'd built a treehouse in the canopy of three ancient pines just across the yard, but now only a few rotted boards clung to the branches of his old den. He'd taken to sleeping up in the treehouse back then instead of the drafty shed, and it was on the uneven porch of his treetop home that the raven had dropped a loop of wire. A rabbit snare.

He hadn't caught a damned thing in it for the next three weeks, but little by little, he taught himself how to read signs for rabbits. Burrows, fur, scat, smell. He'd taught himself where to hang the loops around the burrow exits so that he could find success. And one day, he did. One dead rabbit that said he would survive another few days.

And the raven had been watching with something akin to pride in her eyes.

After that, he'd used that first snare as a template for making nine more. And by the second spring, setting and checking snares became part of his daily routine.

Late in the second year, the raven had dropped off two shiny fishing lures that glinted in the sun. She liked shiny things best. Meat became his main source of food in those early years since gardening didn't come naturally to him. He had struggled to figure out how to get seeds for the next year, and his plants often got yellow patches on the leaves and wouldn't produce. Eventually, he'd figured that out, too.

And his raven sat in her tree, always watching.

By his eleventh birthday, however, not even the raven's presence could keep the loneliness at bay. Wild bears were solitary creatures, but Bear shifters were social by nature, and he had no one. He didn't speak and eventually lost the use of his words until he'd met Creed. Now he had to work constantly at communicating with other people because back then, for so many years, his world had been void of human interactions. Cicadas, crickets, injured rabbits, bullfrogs, howling coyotes...these were thing things that filled up his head. Not the laughter from when Mom and Dad had been alive. Not conversations about how his day had gone or lullabies to help him sleep at night. His human world had dimmed and quieted until there was no need for it anymore. He had no one around to teach him about growing up or how to act around other people. There was no verbal compass for right and wrong, only instinct. And a bear's instincts weren't driven by good and evil. They were driven by want and need.

Why the fuck hadn't she told him then? How many times had he been curled in on himself with hunger? How many times had he been driven to the edge of madness with desperation to hear someone talk to him? To say his name, or tell him everything was going to be okay? How many times had he been bone-deep cold in those snowy winter months and been sure that day would be his last?

Yet, she'd never revealed her human side to him. Aviana had watched and brought him tiny treasures, but she hadn't given him what he really desired—companionship.

And now she was back after all these years, and for what? To reveal herself now after all the damage had been done. After he'd lost his mind, lost control of his bear, and was worthless as a functioning member of society? His thoughts had become clearer and clearer around her. His bear had quieted, and for a minute, he'd felt normal. Like maybe Creed wasn't going to have to put him down. And it had been such a huge relief to feel safe for that instant, because every morning Easton woke up thinking today was going to be his last on this earth. Living in fear for his life like that for too long had ruined him from the inside out.

She could've ended his suffering years ago by Changing and talking to him. By looking at him like she had last night through those big blue eyes, as if he was worth something.

Instead, when he'd needed a friend the most, she'd flown away and left him altogether.

And after she'd gone, out in these woods all alone, Easton's bear had killed the last good parts of him.

TWELVE

Aviana waited for hours, hoping Easton would come back. Her night vision wasn't as good as a bear shifter's, and flying out after him wouldn't work. Not with a sore shoulder, and not without a clear idea of where he had gone.

With the first streaks of dawn, she flew stiffly from the branch she'd been using as a lookout post, Changed into her human form, and stumbled into his trailer. She washed the salty tear streaks from her face, then dressed. There was a first aid kit still in its plastic wrapping under his sink, so she ripped it open and cleaned the bite mark as best she could.

A shrill whistle from the trailer park told her the others were waking up for their workday. She huddled into Easton's jacket and sat on the front porch stairs, waiting.

Willa called out, "I'll get him!" over the sound of truck engines roaring to life.

The sound of dry leaves crackling under footfall traveled to Aviana, and she wrung her hands as she waited for Willa to come. She couldn't face the others right now, so she was grateful it was Willa who was coming to Easton's trailer.

The spunky red-head froze in her tracks when she saw Aviana sitting there. Willa scanned the yard and asked, "Where's Easton? And why do you smell sad?"

Aviana swallowed hard. "Easton's gone."

Willa's eyes went hard as she asked, "Gone where?"

"He turned into his bear and went that way last night," Aviana explained, jerking her chin toward the woods and hiccupping slightly. "I think he hates me." A sob worked its way up her throat, and she clamped her mouth shut, biting her lip hard to punish herself for falling apart like this. Sometimes, she got so tired of herself for being so fucking weak. She turned her head toward Willa, but the stretch of her neck pulled on her injury and she hissed as pain rippled through her shoulder.

"Are you hurt?"

"It's nothing I don't deserve. Willa? Can I ask you something personal?" Easton's bite had been bothering her all night.

Willa sat beside her on the porch stair. "Shoot."

"If a bear shifter bites a woman, what exactly does it mean?"

"Are you fucking kidding me?" Willa reached across her and ripped Easton's jacket to the side, exposing the bandage over her shoulder. Willa ripped into that, too, and stood. "You don't smell like a bear."

"Because I wasn't ever human," she said in a pathetic whisper.

Willa was scary as shit when she was mad, her eyes glowing green like Easton's did when his bear was riled up. "What's going on?"

Aviana's face crumpled, and she wiped her hand across her leaking eyes. "I've known Easton most of his life, but not as a girl. I'm a raven shifter."

The blood drained from Willa's face as she stared at her with those terrifying, glowing eyes. Her voice pitched to a whisper as she asked, "You're Easton's raven?"

Aviana sniffled, and her lip trembled as she nodded. "He's talked about me?"

Willa approached and sank down heavily

beside her. "Yeah. He's mentioned you."

"He didn't know I was a shifter when we were younger. He thought I was just a crow, and it took me a long time to get brave enough to find him. I wanted to wait until I thought he was ready before I told him who I really was, but last night, he bit me. And when I didn't Turn, he started piecing it all together." Aviana sagged against her. "Willa, he was so mad. He said I left him, but it wasn't my choice. Nothing was my choice. I love him. I always have."

"Holy hairy testicles, Crow." Willa draped her arm around Aviana's shoulder and rested her cheek against the top of her head. "That isn't just a bite on your shoulder. It's a claiming mark. Easton's marked you as his mate."

"Oh, my gosh," Aviana said on a breath, sitting up straight and searching Willa's dimming eyes. "He did it before he found out who I was." Easton was probably filled with regret now. Her heart sank even lower. He wouldn't want to keep her now. Not after last night.

"Willa! Easton!" Creed yelled through the trees.

"Aviana, listen to me," Willa said urgently, grabbing her hands. "You can't let Creed see that mark until you find Easton. You both will need to explain everything. He's on thin ice with our alpha, and he disobeyed a direct order to claim you. Do you understand what I'm saying?"

"I need to find Easton."

"Yes. Think, Aviana. Did he say anything or give you any clues? Where would he have gone?"

"Willa!" Creed bellowed.

"Uuuh," Aviana whispered, panicked. "He's been holding onto my trinkets lately." Memories. Flashbacks. She didn't know what went on in Easton's head. Not anymore. Home. Den. The divot in the windowsill she used to drop her treasures. Aviana gasped. "He might have gone to his parents' cabin."

"Are you okay to travel with your injury? You aren't healing like you should."

"Ravens don't heal instantly like bears. I can do it if I fly in a straight line there."

A twig cracked on the trail that connected Easton's singlewide to the rest of Grayland Mobile Park.

"Hurry," Willa urged.

"You won't tell your alpha?"

Willa looked determined. "Let me handle Creed. You just get Easton back here."

With a burst of desperation not to be seen by the dragon-blooded alpha grizzly shifter stomping this way, Aviana Changed into her raven and flapped her wings, ignoring the pain on her left side. Up and up she flew until Willa was only the size of an ant by the pile of Aviana's clothes below her.

The world was green beneath her, covered in pine forest and bisected by rivers that snaked back and forth in gently rolling serpent shapes. Occasional cabins dotted the landscape, but not many lived in this wilderness. She circled once over her family's dilapidated cabin just to get her bearing, and then caught an air current going due east. Many miles separated her childhood home from Easton's, and she hadn't returned since the day Dad had packed them up and taken her away from the boy he saw as a threat to his only daughter.

Still, the way was as familiar to her as her flight feathers. A million times she'd flown this journey when she was a young crow, visiting the broken boy in the woods.

She landed on the gnarled branch of the tree that had always been her landing place before. Now, the branch wasn't thin and covered with tender pine needle shoots. It was aged, thick, and the bark was rough under her grasp.

Easton was there, wearing jeans that hung dangerously low around his narrow hips as he leaned against the battered door of the shed. His back was bare, but the cool March air didn't seem to bother him. Easton had been made for these woods. Carved from them and made invincible by his struggles here.

He turned and looked directly at her over his shoulder. She expected his eyes to be glowing like a demon, but they were dim and sad. The color wasn't the eerie lime green they usually were, but the darker green of mature forest moss.

"Do you know how many times I looked up onto that branch you're clinging to after you left?" His throat moved as he swallowed hard and pushed off the door. He turned and approached, his gate hitched as he limped toward her. "A year. It was a full year before I could convince my stupid eyes to stop checking for you. And now here you are."

Aviana flitted to the ground and Changed. The cool air stung against her bare skin, and she felt completely stripped down and vulnerable in front of him, but she had to tell him the truth now. She had to at least try to explain it wasn't just him who'd been hurt.

"Do you know anything about raven shifters?" Her voice came out frail and weak, just like her.

He shook his head. "I didn't even know you existed. Fuckin' obviously."

"My people aren't like yours, Easton. You are a powerful apex predator shifter while I'm a bad omen."

"I don't understand."

"Do you know how many of my people are shot each year while they are shifted? Just because of the bad luck we represent. It's against our laws, on the punishment of being shunned, that we expose ourselves to anyone." She arched her eyebrows and looked pointedly at him. "*Anyone*. And you aren't just a human or a scavenger shifter, Easton. You're a grizzly, a shifter my people naturally fear. Being with you as a crow was already a huge risk, but I couldn't help myself. I had to be around you, or my life felt empty. Especially out here where I was being raised until I could control my shifts around humans. When your parents died—"

"I don't want to talk about them with you."

"When your parents died, my heart broke for you. I watched the boy I loved hurt and cry out for help, and I couldn't do anything. I couldn't tell my parents you were out here alone. I was scared they would call their council, and they would come out here and put you down. A lone grizzly cub with no people? I couldn't tell anyone what had happened to you. All I could do was try to help you with snares and lures and scraps of food when I could sneak it away from my cabin. I couldn't even carry a damned blanket when you were cold in the winters. Watching you break over those years broke a part of me too."

"Then why did you leave? If you cared so much, why did you leave me here? You were my only friend. God dammit, Ana, there was no one. When you left…there was no one."

"You got caught in that trap. Do you remember?" Aviana clenched her hands and forced her mind back to that awful day. "You were hurt, screaming. Bleeding. I thought you were going to die in that trap, and even in my human form, I was too scrawny to help. You tried and tried to get out of it, and your leg looked so bad." She wiped her eyes again. "I flew back to my house and told my dad. I begged him to help you, and he was so angry. He said I'd betrayed my family and my people by making friends with you. I promised never to see you again if he would just let you out of the trap and not tell the council about you. I led him to you."

"I remember him." Easton crossed his arms over his chest and looked off into the forest with a faraway look in his eyes. "He was tall. Skinny. Fine boned like you are. He pulled the trap off and set my broken bone like he'd done it a hundred times. And then he ripped the trap out of the ground and walked off into the woods with it dangling from his hand and didn't look back. I hadn't seen another person in so long, I thought I'd imagined him. You sent him?"

"I didn't know what else to do. He packed us up that night, and we moved to Rapid City the next day." Aviana was shivering so hard now, her teeth chattered. "Did you find my last gift?"

"The shiny rock?"

She smiled sadly and shook her head. "It wasn't just a shiny rock. It was a diamond. I found it on the ground, and I'd been saving it. It was my favorite possession. My dad said it was worth a lot of money, but I didn't care about selling it. The night before we left, I snuck out and visited your treehouse for the last time. You were curled up inside sleeping with your leg all bandaged. I gave you the diamond because I hoped that someday you would escape this place."

Easton screwed up his face and turned his back to her. He arched his head back and muttered a curse. He linked his hands behind his head before he spun back to her and wrapped her up in a bone-cracking hug. "I didn't know it was valuable, but I wouldn't have sold it even if I had. It's in the box with the rest of the presents you gave me. I didn't know. I didn't know."

Easton's words were muffled against her neck, and she was openly weeping now. She'd been afraid he wasn't ever going to touch her again. He lifted her off her feet, and she nuzzled his face because she loved him so fucking much she couldn't be close enough to him. Not ever.

"Easton, Easton, Easton. I've thought about you all this time. Missed you so badly and compared every potential mate to you. I imagined how it would feel to hold you like this without my feathers."

"You're cold, Ana. You'll get sick. Shit, you're bleeding. Look what I've done to you," he murmured, setting her down, his eyes on her shoulder. The skin was jagged and deeply torn where he'd bitten her, and sure enough, it was weeping red again. The multiple Changes weren't helping.

"I wanted this. Stop fussing with it. It's okay. I wanted you to choose me for a mate someday. I just didn't know that was how it was done with your people. And I certainly didn't know you were going to claim me our first time."

"I hadn't done that before. I messed up."

"You haven't claimed anyone before? I'm glad."

"No. I mean, I've never slept with a woman."

Aviana's mouth dropped open.

A slow smile spread across Easton's face as he pressed his finger under her chin until her mouth closed again. "You'll catch flies."

"Wait, you were a virgin? But you knew exactly what to do, and you were so good at it. You didn't even ask me what I liked. You just knew." Okay, she was rambling but, dear goodness, the man had given her a bona fide orgasm first try. And he was a virgin? "Why didn't you tell me?"

"What difference did it make?" Easton was still smiling.

"I don't know. I could've lit some candles

or taken it slower or…something."

"Yeah, well, lucky you. You got the first Beaston bang, complete with copious amounts of blood, teeth gnashing, and pain. Congratulations."

"You're teasing." She liked that Easton could joke with her after all of the heavy grit that had happened. The smile slipped from Aviana's face. "Can I ask you something?"

Easton rubbed her arms to warm her and nodded.

"If you would've known I was your raven before we slept together, would you have claimed me still?"

"Are you asking if I still want you for my mate?"

She dipped her chin once. His answer meant the world.

"I don't regret my mark on you."

"We have to go back home and explain everything to Creed. He'll understand. He has to. You're mine, and I'm yours, and technically you didn't Turn me, so you didn't disobey his order."

"I thought you said ravens were naturally afraid of bears."

"Yeah, so?"

"So if the Gray Backs scare you, I can claim

my own territory and keep you safe. You won't have to smell scared anymore."

"But you love your crew."

His eyes stayed steady and clear on her, but he didn't answer.

"You'd give them up for my comfort?" she asked, stunned.

"Any good mate would, and since I'll be shit at most of this, it's the least I can do."

Aviana trailed kisses down the line between his taut pecs and rested her cheek against his drumming heartbeat. "Silly man, I'd never ask you to give up something you love just for my comfort. The Gray Backs are growing on me. Take me home, Easton."

Without a word, Easton backed away and kicked out of the too big jeans. With eyes full of adoration, he hunched into himself and exploded into the massive grizzly bear she'd treasured for all these years. She wasn't dumb, or blind. Easton struggled a great deal with his animal side thanks to what he'd endured in this place. But he was still trying, and that spoke volumes about the caliber of man he was.

Easton strode off with powerful steps, his razor sharp claws digging into the earth as he moved away from her. And as he reached the first line of trees, he looked back over his shoulder and waited.

Aviana smiled and Changed into her raven. She beat her wings against the air until she reached the muscular hump between his shoulder blades. Gripping his silver fur in her small talons, she held on as he took off in the direction of the trailer park.

And though years stood between the last time they'd traveled together like this and now, she was filled with that same stomach-fluttering bond she'd built with Easton. She felt the same elation she had when she'd touched his fur for the first time as a raven when they were children. Their history together stretched on and on. No matter what lay ahead of them with Creed, she would be there with Easton, standing beside him, fighting for their second chance.

Because from this day on, she was never going to fly away from her Easton again.

THIRTEEN

Easton brushed his fingertip down each vertebra in her back, almost as if he were counting them. He'd filled up the tub with steaming water as soon as they got back, but the chills wouldn't leave her body. Aviana drew her knees tighter to her chest and rested her cheek on one so she could see him better.

Easton's bright green eyes followed his finger as he started at the top of her spine and started again. He was leaning on the tub, chin resting on his arm, and an absent smile on his lips.

She was marrow-deep exhausted, but Easton had made her a bowl of stew, lit candles in the bathroom, and now seemed content to forgo sleep just to stare at her skin. She understood. Aviana had been drinking him in since she'd first seen him again, too.

"What are you thinking about?" she whispered in a soft voice, afraid to disturb the moment.

"Do you remember when the rabbits got to my vegetable garden?"

She answered his smile with one of her own. God, she loved his dimples. They were even more special since he only seemed to flash them for her. "You were eleven."

Easton sat up and pushed her gently backward until her hair was immersed in the water, then he lifted her out and poured a dollop of shampoo in his palm. As he worked her hair into a lather, he said, "I wanted to snare all the rabbits and put them into a stew with my vegetables."

"But all you caught was a cold from obsessively checking the snares in the middle of the night."

"And you brought me an earring."

Aviana giggled and leaned her head back on his hand in the water, then allowed him to pour a plastic cup over her hair to rinse out the suds. "Not all of my gifts had to mean something, you know."

"But you couldn't bring me cold medicine?"

She giggled harder as she sat up.

"For fuck's sake, a single pain killer would've done wonders for the headache that came along with it. But no. You gave me a shiny earring."

"I like shiny things. That is a high compliment that I can part with them for you. I found it on a hiking trail. For some reason I can't think of now, I thought you would like it. And besides, you're a bear shifter. I thought you weren't supposed to get sick."

"And I haven't since. Damn rabbits cursed me."

She blinked slowly as he traced her backbone again. "Was it awful after I left?"

"Crow, crow, why are you still cold?" he asked in that deep timbre she was still getting used to.

"I'll get stronger. You didn't answer my question."

With a sigh, Easton pulled his shirt over his head. His abs rippled with the movement. After tossing it into the pile with her discarded clothes, he shucked his jeans, too. Slowly, he slid into the bathtub behind her, then pulled her back against his chest and wrapped his arms around her. There was barely any room in the small tub for a man Easton's size, but he didn't seem to mind folding his legs around her.

"Yes." He pressed his forehead against the back of her neck. "But it's done, and I wouldn't change it now."

"You wouldn't?"

"If I would've kept you all my life, I couldn't appreciate you like I do now. I wouldn't know how bad it can hurt without you."

Oh. Aviana closed her eyes and melted back against him. Easton was big and strong and warm. Already her chills were lessening with him curled around her. It had been a long and trying day, and her stamina wasn't great. Not yet. But Easton deserved a strong mate, and she was determined to become better for him.

"Easton?"

"Mmm?" he rumbled, dragging a washrag around the edge of her claiming mark.

"I feel safe with you."

Easton snorted and told her, "Your instincts suck."

She laughed and said, "I'm serious. I've always felt safe around you."

"I bit you the first chance I got."

"Because you wanted to claim me."

"I'm not good, Ana. I'm not."

"You *are*."

He dragged the scruff on his chin across the back of her neck, back and forth, back and forth. His silent argument didn't matter, though. She knew the truth. She saw straight to Easton's soul, and he was good to the core. He just had to learn how to act around other people instead of reacting on grizzly instincts. She understood his quirks and loved each of them.

"Tell me a secret no one else knows," she whispered, trickling water over his knee.

"I want to go somewhere big and far away. Somewhere like the Grand Canyon."

"You do?"

His lips pressed against the back of her neck. "Mmm hmm. When I was a kid, I thought my bear would never let me out of my territory."

"Your parents' land?"

"Yep. He claimed it, and then it got really hard to leave. I still live close, and sometimes I wish I could go somewhere away from here. Stupid. I know I'm not ready. Maybe I won't ever be. Can't keep control. I went to Dodge City to help Jason out last year, and the job took way longer than it was supposed to because I couldn't stay human very long.

Didn't tell my crew that part. Sometimes I just want to see something other than these mountains. Now you. Tell me a secret."

Aviana leaned her head back against his shoulder and smiled. "I used to watch you sleep."

"When?"

"After you'd built that treehouse. I would sneak out late at night after my parents were asleep, and I'd perch on the window where the moonlight made you look blue, and I'd watch you. You always looked so calm in your sleep. Relaxed. Like a kid again. Like you weren't fighting for survival. I wanted to Change and sleep beside you so badly, you can't even imagine. You were warm and felt safe, and I wanted to be under your arm, sleeping with you."

Easton huffed a small chuckle, and she reveled in the vibration against her back. His laughs were for her.

"Easton, about when we slept together before…"

He pulled her wet hair to her other shoulder and kissed gently right beside her bite. It looked awful now, bruised and torn.

"Losing your virginity is a really big deal," she whispered. "Do you want to talk about it?"

"Losing it isn't a big deal to animals."

When a soft growl rattled his chest, delicious chills rippled up her skin. Easton wouldn't talk about it or linger on nostalgic thoughts. She knew he wouldn't. His answer had been a flippant and honest denial that sex for the first time had been life-altering at all. And to her, it made sense. Easton was more animal than man. Her cheeks warmed with happiness as she snuggled back against him.

She'd been his first, and the burning mark on her shoulder said Easton wanted her to be his only.

Easton kissed her bite mark softly, then settled her wet hair back into place. "Ana, I won't ever hurt you when we're mating again. I won't hurt you ever."

His promise brought an emotional smile to her lips. "Okay."

He massaged her breast, dumping instant heat into her middle. His erection had been swollen and hard against her back since he'd slipped into the tub behind her, but now, he rolled his hips slightly. "You like when I touch you here," he murmured, slipping his hand down to cup her sex, right over her clit.

Ana rolled her eyes closed and nodded.

"And here," he said low as he slipped his

finger into her.

Rocking against his touch, she nodded again.

His other arm encircled her stomach and pulled her tight against his dick, standing straight against her spine. Rolling his hips, he pressed against her in the same slow rhythm he fingered her. Pressure built with every stroke, and she slipped her hands behind his head as he kissed her neck. The warm water lapped at her ribs when Easton rested his chin on her shoulder as he brought her closer to climax. A soft moan pushed past her lips as her body pulsed in a fast rhythm around his finger. She still couldn't believe how good he was at touching her. She was almost embarrassed by how fast she came with him, but he didn't seem disappointed.

"Want to feel," he murmured in that gravelly, inhuman timbre that said his bear was close.

Rolling her forward, he settled her on her hands and knees. Easton slid into her slow from behind. She'd never done it like this—like the animals did. But with Easton, it felt right. It felt natural. His powerful body curved over hers as he pushed his thick shaft deep inside of her. He was big and stretched her, but she was ready. Relaxed and wet.

Slowly, he eased back by inches, then thrust into her again. Holy moly, he was sexy—a growl vibrating against her back, him nibbling kisses on her uninjured shoulder. His powerful arm flexed and locked on one side, while his other gripped around her waist. The next thrust was faster. Out slow, in hard. Ana arched her back and gave him a better angle.

"Fffuck," he whispered shakily as he slammed into her again.

Pressure with each stroke. She could climax just thinking about his powerful body covering her. Her middle was tingling now and everything felt so good. Floaty. Numbing. *Lock those arms. Almost there.* "Ah!" she cried as he pushed into her again. "Easton! I'm going to…"

"Come for me," he said on a growl as his hips pumped into her again.

Her body shattered. The pleasure was so intense, she had to close her eyes and focus on not falling apart. The snarl in Easton's throat was constant now as he bucked into her. When her body clenched around him, Easton froze with her name on his lips. Hot, pulsing jets shot into her, filling her, dripping down her thighs as he pulled out. Then he slid back in and emptied himself completely. Her body pulsed on and on, each aftershock as intense as the last as he bucked against her more slowly, drawing each one from her.

The water was getting cold against her arms and legs, but Easton didn't seem in a hurry to sever their connection. His lips gone soft, he ran kisses across her shoulder instead. His teeth grazed her skin in a soft bite every couple of kisses as the pulsing sensation faded completely away. He was so warm, so strong, she couldn't help but feel safe all tucked up under him, even with his teeth brushing her skin. He wouldn't hurt her.

And just as her arms felt as though they wouldn't hold her anymore, Easton slid out of her and stood, dragging her with him. He bent down and folded her into his arms, then stepped out of the tub and carried her to his bed. She smiled languidly at the fresh white sheets he'd put on. No more blood stains from when he'd claimed her, and suddenly it was clear why his bedding looked so clean and soft. He'd obviously spent some money on the thick comforter and crisp linens. They were to banish the memory of all the nights he'd slept on spruce limbs and plucked pillows of grass. The living room might resemble the treehouse he'd made himself all those years ago, but his bedroom…that was his attempt to move on.

Easton settled her in bed and stood beside her with his head canted. He looked at her body as though she was the most beautiful thing he'd ever seen. "I'm going to clean you," he said in a rumbling voice.

She nodded, ready for a soft cloth. But when he lowered himself to the bed and dragged a trail of kisses down her ribs to her stomach, it became abundantly clear what kind of cleaning Easton had in mind. Ana held in a giggle. She should've known.

Her mate laved his tongue up her still wet folds, and drew a soft sigh from her lips. He was meticulous and rhythmic, and now he was definitely conjuring another orgasm. Ana bent her legs and gripped his hair. Easton's eyes glowed green as he looked up at her, and with only a second of hesitation, he gave into her silent pleading and slipped his tongue inside of her.

Ana moaned helplessly at how good he felt right there. Easton grabbed her hips and dragged her closer, then drove his tongue deeper. Arching her back, she cried out and clenched his hair. His head bobbed between her legs as he drove her closer and closer to climax. "Easton," she yelped as her body clenched around his tongue in quick, throbbing orgasm. He licked her until she twitched and lay exhausted and spent. Easton kissed the insides of her thighs gently, then climbed up beside her and pulled her against his chest. He pulled the covers over them, then leaned his chin on top of her head. His dick was long and hard against her belly, but he didn't move to relieve himself in her. Instead, he murmured, "Sleep now, mate."

Mate. She smiled and nuzzled closer to him.

And finally...*finally*...after all those years of wanting, she got to sleep safe and warm under the arm of the man she loved.

FOURTEEN

"Don't smell scared," Easton said, his eyes blazing as he cast her a quick glance.

"I can't help it." Aviana clutched tight to his hand as Easton led her toward the Grayland Mobile Park. "Your crew is intimidating. All bear shifters are really."

"Yet you are mated to Beaston," he muttered so low, she almost didn't hear it.

She frowned at the use of that name. Sure, his animal was in control, but that was because of what he'd been through. That bear inside of him also was to thank for his survival. Easton had lost his family when he was just a kid, then eked out a life in the woods all alone. "You say Beaston like it's a bad name, but I think it's fucking awesome," she said defiantly.

He cast her a startled glance and skidded to a stop. "Why?"

"Because you might be a beast, Easton Novak, but you are also a survivor, and I'm so fucking proud of how far you've come, I can hardly stand it. So don't utter that name around me unless you are owning it. Badass, snarly, scary-eyed mountain man who protects the heart of a fearful raven. You *are* Beaston. My Beaston."

A slow smile had spread across his face as she'd ranted, and now his dimples showed. "Okay," he said low, pulling her into a hug. "I'm Beaston."

A sharp whistle trilled across the valley. Creed was letting them know it was time for the crew to head up to the mountains to clear timber, but they would have to wait. She and Easton had an announcement to make before he went to work.

The Gray Backs were all gathered near the bricked-in fire pit talking when Easton led her out of the tree line.

"There they are," Willa called, looking relieved. "Now we can have someone unbiased settle the score," she said, looking pointedly at Gia. Georgia was rifling through a backpack sitting on a food prep table near them, and she shook her head, though she was still smiling.

"What is it?" Aviana asked, voice small and

pathetic. With a frown, she said louder, "What is it?"

Easton looked at her proudly.

"Dude, Beaston's holding her hand," Matt said low to Jason.

Willa kicked her mate's boot and held out both hands as they approached. In one was a pile of green M&Ms and in the other was a pile of orange. "Which ones are supposed to make you horny, green or orange?"

Aviana snorted and tried to think back on her school days. "I think it's green makes you horny."

"Here, Griz, eat these," Willa said, dumping the green pile into Matt's hand.

He snorted and popped them all in his mouth. "I can't even believe you want me hornier than I already am," he said around the mouthful of candy.

"So it's orange to make your boobs big then," Gia said matter-of-factly. "Told you."

Aviana laughed and asked, "Can I have some orange ones then?"

With a big toothy grin, Willa handed her half the pile of oranges and poured the other half into her maw.

Easton slapped the candy out of Aviana's hands with a look of panic in his eyes. "Don't want bigger boobs on you. Too much."

Aviana stood there stunned, looking at the bright colored chocolates scattered across the white gravel road.

Jason was laughing now, hands around his stomach, bent over, wheezing. "Dude, it's not real."

"Oh," Easton said with a confused frown as he watched Jason fall over onto the ground, kicking his legs as he laughed. He swung his troubled gaze to Aviana and murmured, "Sorry."

She was trying not to laugh, really she was, but Easton was so fucking cute. Sexy as all get-out, eyes wild and bright as he made sure she stayed just as she was. If she'd had any question that her flat chest bothered her mate before, it was dispelled now.

"Why are you eating M&Ms for breakfast?" she asked.

"Gia craves them all the time," Georgia explained. "Willa just mooches them."

"I help her eat them," Willa corrected. "It's not mooching if I'm doing it out of the goodness of my heart."

Creed was quiet beside Matt, shaking his head and looking tired, as if his crew already exhausted him.

"I have something to say," Easton announced in a strong, formal voice.

Jason kicked into a star shape on the ground and looked at Easton, upside down. "That sounds serious."

"It is." Easton lifted his gaze to Creed and cocked his head, exposing his neck. "I have to beg your forgiveness."

Creed stood straighter as his black eyes lightened to a gray that matched the early morning sky. "What did you do?"

Aviana couldn't even look at him like this. Not when Creed was making the air so heavy. It was hard to draw a breath under his stare, so she angled her chin down and looked at Willa instead.

"As Second, I forbid you to bleed him," Willa said, standing to her full height of not even five foot tall and glaring at Creed.

"What?" Creed asked, looking even angrier. "It doesn't work like that. You're second, not alpha. What's going on?"

"Show him," Easton murmured, nudging Aviana's shoulder.

Aviana pulled her stretchy pink cotton shirt to the side and exposed the tattered flesh of Easton's claiming mark.

Creed's dark eyebrows jacked up, and he

swung a dangerous glare at Easton. "What the fuck did you do?"

"I'd say either a zombie bit her or Easton claimed her," Willa said helpfully as she dug around in the crinkly package of M&M's for more candy.

"Enough!" Creed yelled.

Willa didn't even look cowed, but damn what the electricity in the alpha's voice did to Aviana. With a grunt, she fell to her knees under the heaviness of the stomach-curdling anger Creed was throwing off in waves.

Easton looked down at her then back to Creed, eyes blazing as a low, menacing rumble rattled his throat. "Let her up."

"You Turned her?" Creed bellowed. "After I forbid it, you Turned her?"

"She doesn't smell like a bear," Georgia whispered from near the table where she looked like she was struggling to stay upright, too.

"It took you all of what...a day? A day to disobey a direct order?" Creed said, hands on his hips. "What the fuck, man?"

"She's mine."

"You just met her!"

"Let her up!" Easton yelled, voice gone snarly.

"Oh, for shit's sake," Willa said, "Aviana, move your tail feathers, girl. Fuck Noggin's about to Change."

Creed hunched into himself just as Willa rushed Aviana. Easton's silver bear exploded from him in the exact moment a huge black bruin grizzly ripped out of Creed.

"No! Don't hurt him!" she cried as Willa dragged her by the waist over the gravel.

"Stay there," Willa ordered, eyes hard. Two seconds later, a brown bear burst from her skin, and when Aviana looked up, Creed and Easton clashed so hard the earth under her feet shook. Jason was scrambling out of the way, and a light-colored grizzly was already hovering protectively between him and the battling bears. Georgia?

The sheer violence of the bear fight held Aviana stunned in place. Creed and Easton slashed each other with resounding, clawed slaps. Roaring, growling, biting. Bleeding. The white gravel was being painted with red.

Even with Willa trying to maneuver between them and Matt Changing into a red, scarred-up grizzly to help, Easton and Creed only had eyes for maiming each other.

She had to do something.

With a pop and flapping wings, Aviana

Changed and dive-bombed Creed. She pecked his ear and few out of slapping range, then circled around.

"Creed, she isn't a bear!" Gia screamed. "Creed, stop!"

Aviana tucked her wings and dove for the black grizzly again, but this time, she didn't get to touch him. This time he turned at the last moment and swatted her out of the air. With a terrified caw in her throat, she hit the grass hard.

Gia was running for her now, round belly leading her. She fell to her knees beside Aviana and picked her up gently. "Oh no," she whispered, pulling her carefully to her soft bosom. With a look of pure human fury, she stood and turned to the bears battling. "Creed Joseph Barnett! You're hurting me!" she screamed.

Creed's onyx colored bear immediately shrank into the dark-haired, silver-eyed man. With a pained grunt, he fell forward onto his hands and knees on the gravel road. Willa and Matt rushed Easton, trying to keep him from murdering the alpha in human form.

"What?" Creed asked as he struggled up and stared in confusion at his mate. "How am I hurting *you*?"

"Because look what you're fighting over!" Gia shoved Aviana forward.

"Caw!" Aviana said helpfully. Translation: *I'm a fucking crow! Not a Turned bear shifter.*

Creed stared at her like he'd never seen a bird in his life. "I...I don't understand."

When Easton took a swipe too close to him, Creed ducked neatly out of the way and yelled, "Easton, Change back!"

Easton's roar died in his throat as he fell to his knees and shrank into his human skin. A pained grimace was on his face, but it didn't stop the death glare for Creed. "I didn't Turn her. She wasn't ever human. And if you would've fucking listened, I would've had time to explain that I've known her all my life. And I swear on my den, if you hurt her, I'm going to fucking bleed you, Gray Back."

Jason stood to the side, arms crossed over his chest, looking grumpy. "That insult still doesn't make any sense, Beaston. We're all Gray Backs!"

Willa shrank back into her naked human skin and kicked the gravel. "God dammit, Creed!"

Matt was now a giant, naked human with scars all over his torso. "Did he hurt you?" he asked, worry in his deep voice.

"No! He spilled all my M&M's!"

"Oh, for fuck's sake," Creed said. "Someone explain to me what is going on."

Willa stomped her foot. "Creed, meet Easton's childhood friend who is a raven shifter, but only Easton didn't know she was a raven shifter until yesterday when he gave her a claiming mark while they were boinking and she didn't Turn. He got mad, he ran off, that's why he wasn't at work yesterday, and now you just B-slapped the bird he's in love with. You deserve that scar," she said, jamming a finger at the long claw mark across Creed's chest that was dripping red.

"You," the alpha said, pointing at Aviana. "Change back."

"You can't tell her what to do," Easton snarled.

"I can so. She's a Gray Back now."

"Aaaw," Willa said, clasping her hands in front of her chest and shrugging her shoulders with a mushy smile on her face. "The final Gray Back."

Creed stared at her until she had the good sense to drop her gaze to her feet.

"Now please," Creed gritted out, "Change back so I can properly apologize."

In a flush of absolute mortification, Aviana

flew out of Gia's hands and landed on the ground, then shifted into her human form.

"Boobs," Willa sang in a barely audible voice, only to be glared at by Creed again.

Jason snorted from behind the blond grizzly that was still standing protectively in front of him. He cleared his throat and apologized when Creed tossed him an annoyed glance.

With a sigh, Creed hooked his hands on his naked hips and said, "Aviana, I wholeheartedly apologize for my actions here today. I should've listened better before I punished Easton, and I'm sorry if you got hurt in that fight." His shoulders lifted and fell in a heavy sigh. "Welcome to the most fucked up crew of shifters that ever walked these mountains."

"C-team!" Willa said, shaking her hands like cheerleader pom-poms.

Most of the Gray Backs were naked and bleeding, and Georgia the Scary Bear was now licking the back of Jason's smiling head until his dark hair stood up in all directions. Most of them were smiling despite the violence that had just occurred, and all were staring at Aviana who was hiding her tits behind her arm and doing her best to cover her honey pot with an oak leaf she'd hurriedly plucked from the ground.

Her mouth was hanging open, but she snapped it closed and swallowed hard. In a tiny voice, she said, "Thank you?"

"Uuuh, Willa?" Gia said in a strange tone beside her. "You were wrong. Aviana's not the final Gray Back."

"What do you mean?" Creed asked, worry slashing through his churning, silver eyes.

Gia looked at a damp stream that was trailing down the inside legs of her jeans. "I think my water just broke."

FIFTEEN

Easton paced the small waiting room, biting the end of his nail as he checked the window for the eight-hundredth time in the direction of Gia's hospital room.

Aviana understood. He'd watched helplessly as his mother had died during childbirth, and now Gia was having a baby.

His snarling and pacing had already scared off the humans in the waiting room, so now it was just Aviana and the rest of the Gray Backs, minus Creed and Gia, a vending machine that was now fresh out of M&Ms, and an old, scratchy cartoon playing on the small television in the corner.

"I should be in there," Easton rumbled.

"No," Aviana said. "Gia and Creed have to do this on their own. There are doctors and nurses who know exactly what they are doing. She'll be all right."

"But it's taking so long."

"It usually does for a first baby," Willa said from the corner where she had her feet draped across Matt's lap. "She's tough. Gia will be okay."

But even Willa looked worried. Easton's pacing had everyone unsettled.

Easton skidded to a stop, threw the door open, and then bolted into the hallway. They all stood to see Creed coming toward them with a big grin on his face. Aviana drifted to the window to watch Easton talk to his alpha. Creed gripped his shoulder and talked through his smile, and little by little Easton relaxed. And when he finally looked back at Aviana, his bright green eyes held relief. Her heart stopped at how beautiful he was.

Easton jogged back to her and pulled her hand, leading her out of the waiting area and toward Gia's room. "Hurry, Ana. Creed said I could see her first if we hurry."

Aviana's vision was blurring with tears because her Easton was happy. She could feel it coming off him in waves.

Just outside the hospital room, Creed turned to the others and murmured, "Give us a minute." Then he pushed open the door and ushered Easton and Aviana inside.

Gia sat on the bed, comfortable looking and eyes only for the tiny bundle in her arms. She smiled emotionally when she looked up, and Easton sat gently on her bed and tucked her disheveled hair behind her ear.

"Oh, mighty little human, look what you've done," Easton said, his eyes dipping to the sweet baby. He pulled Aviana closer and moved the blanket farther away from the sleeping babe's face. "Look at her," he said on a breath. "Perfect in every way. Gia, Gia, Gia, good mommy."

Gia's shoulders were shaking now, and she was sniffling as she rested her head against Easton's shoulder. Creed stood on her other side, leaning over the baby with the proudest look in his dark eyes.

"Do you want to hold her?" she whispered thickly to Easton.

His eyes went wide, but he nodded and held his arms out. Gia set the tiny baby gently in the cradle of his arms.

Behind them, the rest of the crew filed in and surrounded Gia's bed with *oohs* and *aahs* at the tiny, blanketed girl in Easton's arms.

Slowly, Easton leaned down and smelled the baby's breath. "What do you call her?"

"Rowan," Creed said proudly.

"A right proper name for a little grizzly," Willa said, leaning over Easton's shoulder.

Easton looked up at Creed with a curious, knowing smile spreading across his lips. "She's not a grizzly."

"What?" Gia asked, eyebrows furrowed. "She's Creed's."

"Oh, one look at the creature she's harboring, and no one will ever question it. She'll be a true Gray Back. A fire-breather with silver scales, descended from the last mortal dragon, Creed's grandfather."

"Can't be," Creed said on a breath. "She has too much grizzly and not enough dragon blood in her."

Easton smiled at the baby as he rocked her in his arms. "I had a dream about her. Silver eyes and silver scales."

"A dream," Matt said, sounding unconvinced.

Aviana grinned slow, knowing Easton was right. Her mate was more sensitive to things beyond this world, just like his mother had been.

"Don't believe me?" Easton asked softly. Back and forth, back and forth he rocked the sleeping newborn. "Then smell the dragon's fire on her breath."

SIXTEEN

Last night was the last time she would sleep in this old house. Aviana zipped up her suitcase and pulled it off the rickety bed she'd slept in as a child. Inhaling deeply, she took one last look at the tiny cabin she'd shared with her parents all those years ago. As a child, this place had seemed huge, but that's what childhood memories did. They warped reality, making everything seem bigger and grander from such a small point of view.

Tonight, she would be moving into an old singlewide trailer in the Grayland Mobile Park that the girls called "ten-ten" and swore was magic. She didn't know what she was going to do there yet. Maybe she would teach shifter school when Rowan and the Ashe Crew kids were older. Or perhaps she would help Easton sell his knives and firewood. Or maybe she would reinvent herself completely and start a new adventure. She didn't know. All she knew was that whatever happened next, it would be beside Easton.

Aviana set her suitcase by the door and pulled her cell out of her purse. She'd charged it in the car until the batteries were full because this call couldn't get cut off. It was too important.

The floorboards of the porch creaked as she settled onto the top stair, and looked over the overgrown front yard. She kicked a rusted, bent nail with her flip-flop, thinking about what she would say to the people whose opinion meant the world to her.

How did she tell her parents she'd turned her back on her people?

Licking her lips, she scrolled through her contacts and found the number labeled *Home*. She made the call and bit her thumbnail as she listened to it ring and watched a trio of birds flit across the tall grass.

"Hello?" Dad answered.

"Dad?"

"Oooh, baby. What have you done?" Static blasted across the line, and Dad called in a muffled voice, "Marta, it's her. Pick up the other line."

The line clicked. "Aviana?" Mom asked.

"Hi, Mom."

"Honey, are you okay?"

"Yes, yes, I'm fine. More than fine. I just… I have to tell you both something important."

The line went quiet. Aviana's pulse pounded hard thinking about how thoroughly she was about to break their hearts. Their only child, denouncing her people for a crew of bears.

"Go ahead," Dad said low.

Aviana swallowed hard and blew out a long, shaky breath. "Mom, Dad, I found Easton. I told Caden no on the courtship because the cub I knew all those years ago has grown into a good man. A man who will make me happy and give me a life full of love. I belong with him." Her throat tightened over the words. "I belong with Easton and his people."

"Oh, honey," Mom said, "we know."

Perhaps Aviana had heard her wrong. "I'm sorry…what?"

"Caden sent some of his people to watch you. He forwarded us a picture of you sitting in a bar with a man with green eyes. Your father recognized him right away."

"You knew?"

"We just wanted to give you a chance to tell us when you were ready," Mom said.

Dad was so quiet though, he must be angry. That's how he got when he was really mad. He holed up into himself where no one could reach him.

"Dad, I'm sorry."

"No, baby," Dad said, his words broken. "I'm the one who's sorry. I pulled you away from that boy when I knew you'd bonded with him. Even as young as you were, you cared deeply for him, and I didn't listen. I watched you wither for years. I watched you never connect with any of our people. I watched your face when we got the news that Caden wanted to court you. I hoped you would be happy, but you had this doomed look in your eyes. It's something a parent never wants to see in their child. I was wrong to separate you from Easton. And I hope…" Dad cleared his throat. More softly, he said, "I hope that someday you can forgive me."

Aviana bit her lip so hard she tasted iron. She couldn't fall apart now. "Dad, there's nothing to forgive. I love you both so much. I know you'll have to stop talking to me after I'm shunned—"

"Oh, no we won't," Mom said defiantly. "Honey, we've already been shunned."

"What?"

"We told Caden where he could shove his threats, and it was where the sun don't shine. It was a decision we both made solely based on that picture."

"Why did you do that?"

"Because," Dad said, "in the picture you were smiling like we haven't seen you do since you were a kid. If our people want to banish us for supporting our daughter's happiness, so be it. Living an empty life with Caden isn't what we want for you. We want that smile you had in the picture. The one you get with Easton."

All choked up by her parents' sacrifice, Aviana asked, "Will you visit me? I want you to meet all of the Gray Backs. They're lovely, and so nice. Scary, but protective and fierce, and the women are so important in this crew. I feel stronger. And my alpha and his mate have a brand new baby. Oh, she's so tiny and cute. And I want you to meet the man I've fallen in love with. Easton is wild and powerful, but he's also sweet and takes care of me. He makes me happy. I want you to see how he's turned out, and then you won't have to worry about me living with bears anymore. He protects me. Always."

She could hear the smile in Mom's voice when she said, "Of course. We can't wait to meet Easton and all of your new crew."

"Yes," Dad murmured. "We're looking forward to seeing the old cabin again and seeing you with your...mate. Bear pairs are called mates, right?"

Aviana laughed thickly and hugged the phone tighter to her ear. "Yes." It still made her giddy to hear that word.

"We're happy you've found your place, Aviana," Mom said, sounding proud. "Our brave little raven. We love you."

"I love you both, too. So much."

"Okay, honey. We'll talk soon. Let us know when you settle enough for visitors."

"I will."

"Bye-bye now," Dad said.

"Bye," Aviana said on a happy sigh before she hung up.

She smiled down at the screen of her phone for a long time, looking at her reflection. It *was* there. Dad was right. It was a smile she didn't remember seeing before. A toothy one, given freely and easily. One conjured by the joy Easton had put back into her heart. Her parents had been shunned because of her decision to chase love, yet they hadn't made her feel guilty over it. Instead, they'd been happy that she'd found what she'd been searching for.

Excited, Aviana ran back inside and grabbed the handle of her suitcase. After one last look around the cabin, she closed the door and dragged her luggage to her car.

The Gray Back Crew was cooking a big meal tonight. Hot wings with beer to celebrate her moving into 1010. Now she didn't have to go with a heavy heart that she'd hurt her parents. She could her life with her new crew and the man she loved.

Now, her future with Easton stretched on and on.

She was free.

****

Aviana searched the woods for her Easton to make sure he hadn't gotten off work early, but the woods were empty save the evening birds flitting back to their nests and the cicadas singing their rattling song. This was the game. Sneaking little trinkets for her love, surprise gifts to make up for the years she hadn't been able to find shiny presents and give them to him. Today, she'd found a silver bead along a hiking trail miles away.

Easton always gave her dimple smiles when she found him something to tuck away in his tackle box of treasures under his bed.

In the last two weeks, Aviana had settled into life at the Grayland Mobile Park. Creed and Gia were now parenting tiny Rowan, and the Gray Backs were all smitten. Willa had her worm farm in full swing for the fishing season, and Georgia had her woods to protect. Evenings were spent eating together as a crew and laughing into the night. Yesterday, Easton had shared with his beloved Gray Backs the story of how he'd slowly lost his humanity, and there had been not a single dry eye as he finished with how he'd felt the day he'd found out Aviana was his raven.

She was so damned proud of her brave broken bear.

The Gray Backs still fought like titans and bled each other regularly, but that was unlikely to ever change. It's just how her crew was, but that didn't mean they didn't care about each other. These people, who she'd been so afraid of all her life, would die for each other in a heartbeat. And now she was included in that circle of safety. In the same measure, she would give anything for her people, whom she'd grown to love indescribably much.

Shiny silver bead in her beak, Aviana swooped down to the windowsill where she always dropped his gifts. It was the single window to his workshop, just like the sill she'd dropped that first folded paperclip onto. It had a small split in the wood for balancing round objects, and as she landed on the ledge to drop her treasure there, she drew up short.

There was already something silver and shiny in the crease.

The bead fell from her mouth and rolled to the ground as she realized what it was.

It was a ring.

Glittering diamonds encircled the band, and in the center setting was a gift she would never forget. It was the diamond she'd given him all those years ago—her final present before she'd left.

She scanned the woods, and her gaze landed on Easton, leaning against a tree as if he'd been there all along, arms crossed and eyes glowing in the waning evening light.

Aviana pushed off the window ledge and tucked her crow away into her human skin. "Easton," she whispered, tears burning her eyes.

Slowly, he approached, eyes never leaving hers. With a slight smile, he plucked the ring from the windowsill and dropped to both knees in the dirt.

"You saved me—"

"I didn't." He'd saved himself.

"You *did*." His eyebrows lifted as he leveled her with a serious look. "You are patient and caring and understanding, even when I'm confused. You go out of your way to make me feel cared for and appreciated." He swallowed hard and lifted the ring. "I never want you to leave me again."

Aviana fell forward and hugged his shoulders up tight. "I would never leave you, Easton. You're mine."

He rocked her gently, rubbing her back. "Soft and full of tears," he whispered.

"It's too much," she murmured as she eased back and looked at the ring.

"It's not. You like shiny things, and I told you, I have the means to take care of you. What do you say, Ana? Will you marry me?"

An emotional smile stretched her face, and she nodded as the first tear slipped to her cheek. "Yes, Easton. I'll marry you."

"I'll make you happy," he promised as he slipped the ring onto her finger. "I'll always keep trying to be better for you."

She shook her head and cupped his cheeks, lifting his wild gaze to hers. "You're already perfect for me."

SEVENTEEN

Nerves fluttered in Aviana's stomach like butterfly wings. "You look grumpy."

Easton's frown deepened as he hooked his arm over the steering wheel of his pickup and gassed it up a steep hill. "I just don't understand why those assholes couldn't wait five minutes. I told them I was running late."

Yeah, he'd been late because she might or might not have hidden all his work jeans in the back of his closet. She'd needed to buy the crew a little bit more time, though, so desperate times and measures and all.

"Are you sure you aren't going to get bored today?" he asked. "It's hot, and watching us strip lumber won't be any fun. And why are you wearing those contraptions?" He looked pointedly at her wedge heels she'd worn to match her pastel pink sundress.

"I want to look pretty for you."

"Ana, you look pretty in whatever you wear. Those pokey shoes aren't safe to wear out on the landing. You could break an ankle. And put a hard hat on." His bear growled a long rattling sound in his chest as he reached into his back seat, then handed her a yellow hat. He dragged his gaze back to the switchback he was maneuvering and added, "Please."

She was trying her best to hide a smile. Easton was overprotective, no matter how hard he tried not to be. His bear's instincts got kicked up easily, and she secretly adored that he fussed over her safety.

She did as he asked and settled the hat on her head. It was going to mess up her curls, but that was okay. Pursing her lips, she fiddled with her engagement ring, twisting it back and forth. She couldn't help but watch him. They were almost there, and all of the secret hard work was about to pay off. She hoped.

Easton shot her a suspicious glance, then pulled his attention back to the last big hill before they reached the landing. When the old Ford crested the top, Easton eased off the gas as his eyes went round.

The landing was full of people, all waiting

for him.

"What is this?" he asked as he pulled to a stop in front of the crowd.

"They're all here for you."

"For me?"

She swallowed her emotions down and whispered, "Today is our wedding day."

Easton let off a small gasp and blinked hard at her before he looked at their wedding guests again. "Did you beg them to come?"

"No, Easton. They came because they care about you."

He pushed open the door and stood beside his truck, staring at the crowd and looking shocked to his bones.

Mom was crying from where she and Dad stood with the Gray Backs, front and center. Willa let off a shrill whistle and began clapping. The others joined in, cheering and whooping. Tagan and his Ashe Crew were there behind the Gray Backs, along with Kong and his Lowlanders and Harrison and his Boarlanders. Even Clinton was there with his new crew, looking emotional as he clapped with the others. Damon Daye stood off to the side, holding his great-granddaughter, Rowan, as Creed stood beside him, smiling proudly at Easton.

Aviana walked around the front of the truck and nudged his side. "What do you say? You want to marry me today?"

Easton was nodding over and over as his eyes rimmed with emotion.

"Good," she said, tugging his hand toward the Ashe Crew's alpha. Tagan was certified to perform ceremonies, and when she'd braved the Asheland Mobile Park to ask him to officiate the wedding, he and his crew had offered to help her and the Gray Backs plan everything.

She wiped her damp lashes with the back of her hand as she led Easton to the edge of the landing where her parents had decorated the machinery with white ribbons and oversized bouquets of wildflowers.

"Before we start," Tagan said, "your alpha wants to say a few words."

Creed stepped forward and cleared his throat. "Easton, from the day you asked me to take you into my crew, I knew you were special. I knew you had greatness in you. When I came up with our name, the Gray Backs, I named us for you and your silver bear because I knew you had potential to be the best of us if you just put in the work. And over the past couple of years, I've watched you grow and open up in ways that I couldn't imagine when I first saw you, wild-eyed and barely in control. And now you've found Ana, and I'm so damned proud when I see how well you treat her. How hard you try with the rest of us now." Creed nodded, dark eyes filling. "And today, I can say I was right. You really are the best of us. You turned out to be one of my best friends and a man I admire deeply for never giving up. I'm so happy for you, man." His voice cracked on the last word, and he turned as Gia handed him a thick brown envelope.

As Creed ripped open the sealed flap, Easton hugged Aviana tightly against his side and seemed completely overwhelmed with emotion as he tossed her hardhat to the ground. He kissed her hairline and let his lips linger there.

"Easton, your mate came to me and told me you've always wanted to visit someplace far away. And I know you don't think you're ready to go alone, or even just with Aviana, but we all chipped in and…well…here." He handed Easton the opened envelope.

Easton's chin trembled as he pulled the itinerary out and scanned the first couple of pages. "The Grand Canyon?" he whispered as he lifted a disbelieving gaze to Creed.

"We're all going with you, man. All of your crew. Your people. Your friends. We'll take you there and make sure you stay in control. Damon has given us the entire week off, so we're leaving tomorrow morning. Easton…" Creed said, gripping his shoulders and shaking him slowly. "It's going to be amazing."

"Oh, man. I just—far away?" Easton fumbled his words as he hugged Creed hard and clapped him on the back. "Thank you."

"All right, let's get these two hitched," Tagan said through a grin. "The reception barbecue is getting cold."

Aviana laughed thickly and squared her shoulders up to Easton, then took his hands in hers. *You ready*, she mouthed.

Easton's glowing eyes were certain as he nodded.

Tagan's words were loud and clear, echoing across the landing when he said, "We are gathered here today to witness the matrimony of Aviana King and Easton Novak."

"No," her mate said low, searching her eyes. "It's not Easton." A slow smile spread across his face. "It's Beaston."

Want More of the Gray Backs?

The Complete Series is Available Now

Up Next

Lowlander Silverback
(Gray Back Bears, Book 5)

About the Author

T.S. Joyce is devoted to bringing hot shifter romances to readers. Hungry alpha males are her calling card, and the wilder the men, the more she'll make them pour their hearts out. She werebear swears there'll be no swooning heroines in her books. It takes tough-as-nails women to handle her shifters.

Experienced at handling an alpha male of her own, she lives in a tiny town, outside of a tiny city, and devotes her life to writing big stories. Foodie, wolf whisperer, ninja, thief of tiny bottles of awesome smelling hotel shampoo, nap connoisseur, movie fanatic, and zombie slayer, and most of this bio is true.

Bear Shifters? Check
Smoldering Alpha Hotness? Double Check
Sexy Scenes? Fasten up your girdles, ladies and gents, it's gonna to be a wild ride.

For more information on T. S. Joyce's work,
visit her website at
www.tsjoycewrites.wordpress.com

Manufactured by Amazon.ca
Bolton, ON